INVESTIGATION ENVY

MEL TAYLOR

SEVERN RIVER PUBLISHING

Severn River Publishing
www.SevernRiverBooks.com

ISBN: 978-1-64875-560-6 (Paperback)

ALSO BY MEL TAYLOR

The Frank Tower Mystery Series

Investigation Con

Investigation Wrath

Investigation Greed

Investigation Envy

To find out more about Mel Taylor and his books, visit

severnriverbooks.com/authors/mel-taylor

1

A small dot on the wall kept him alive.

For now.

Preston Wakefield gathered up all the spit he could muster and held the precious liquid there, caught up in his mouth as if this were his last swallow. He could not remember the last time he had a drink of water. The ropes and tape held him firmly to the metal chair. More tape wrapped around his ankles. A belt, looped around his neck and connected somewhere on the wall, meant one wrong move and he would choke.

Wakefield's eyes were free to look about the room. He was tired. Very tired. Every attempt he made to sleep was met with a booming cacophony of loud music. Songs he did not recognize. Two large speakers were stacked in one corner. The blare was only meant to torment him into staying awake. Since no one appeared to complain about the noise, yelling for help was not an option. The extreme lack of sleep made any chance to craft an escape plan futile, and ended up being just a jumbled mess of mismanaged thoughts, lost in the fog. He was worn out almost to the point of being delusional.

The only constant right now was the black dot on the wall.

The dot did not give pain.

The mark gave him a way to focus, remember family, and place some hope that some way, somehow, someone might give thought to the fact he was among the missing and look for him.

When he was first hustled to the room and thrown into the chair, he brushed his thumb against the wall. The round smudge was now his only companion.

Unfortunately, the dot was not a clock. He had no earthly idea of what time it was or how many days he had been in the room. His only respite now was being unhooked for a short time to use a dirty bucket for a restroom. Then he was returned to the chair. Was it one man? Two attackers? It was all hazy.

No one spoke to him. All the directives were a push in the back, a hand gesture on which direction to move, or, to prove a point, a brutal kick to his right side.

Now, Wakefield just wanted to sleep.

He wanted a few moments to close his eyes and let his body rest. Just a few minutes, that was all. Sheer exhaustion caused his body to shut down. It was time to doze.

"Wake up!" The voice came from his right. Not the regular human sound. The voice was mechanical, like a robot. No volume pumped up to the full music. This time, the thing that opened his eyes was a hard slap on the right side of his face.

"I said wake up, dammit!"

Wakefield heard someone speak to him for the first time since his capture. He only had enough strength to open his eyes halfway. Then came another slap. He was awake.

The voice sounds were coming out of a box-type contraption on the man's chest. Each word was computer-like, devoid of emotion, and demanded Wakefield's attention.

He felt hands unwrapping his bonds. The rope and tape were coming off. There was an opening where he could do something, yet he was so weak, a counterattack was near impossible. He was being picked up and moved to a table. A gurney device where his arms and legs were again locked into place with restraints. His view consisted of the dirty ceiling tiles. He was moved down a long hallway and into another room. There were no windows.

He closed his eyes to block a bright light from overhead. Curiosity made him take a longer look. On the wall, he saw a row of knives, each one a different size. Panic moved through him, the adrenalin shocking his brain to contemplate terrible consequences. Wakefield's legs pushed against the restraints in an effort to get up. He jerked on the wrist and chest straps. From deep within him, he let out a guttural yell.

The figure stood there, watching. A hard-surface mask gave no indication of the person inside. Wakefield wrestled and the figure just watched, as if enjoying this weak attempt. The gloved hands picked out a scalpel-looking blade from the wall and approached Wakefield.

Before the figure got any closer, Wakefield pleaded, "Stop what you're doing. Let me go. I won't tell anyone."

"You sure about that?" The mechanical voice was soothing. "There, there. Stop moving or I will have to give you something. But I want you awake for this."

Wakefield wondered about the mask. The thought gave credence to the possibility he knew his attacker. Maybe that was also the reason for masking the voice. He tried to gather facts to give the attacker a name.

Seconds later, Wakefield watched the sharp edge come closer to him until a piece of clothing was cut away, exposing the rapid rise and fall of his chest. His breathing was out of control.

The figure bent down closer, bringing the scalpel blade just an inch from his skin. "Don't worry. It's almost over."

2

Frank Tower tossed the envelope on the stack. Four envelopes in all, each containing an invoice for work done in the past month. There was a bill for six days of surveillance work, tracking down a key defense witness in an upcoming murder trial. The witness was reluctant to testify and yet vital to the case. After two long evenings at a bar, Tower, following a tip, caught up with the man and watched him to make sure it was the right person. Score one for Frank Tower Private Investigations.

There were two more invoices for doing background checks on potential employees at a security firm. And the fourth was finding a deadbeat dad who owed more than one-hundred thousand dollars in payments. On this job, Tower worked for free, pro bono. Monday morning business stuff.

He turned up the smooth jazz emanating from his radio and started to apply stamps to the envelopes when there was a knock on the door.

"Mark David. Am I in trouble?" Tower smiled and cracked the door open to a familiar face. David was his former partner when Tower was on the Stilton Bay police force.

"Ya got a minute?" Mark David walked in before the door was fully opened. A woman followed him. She kept her eyes down at first, only lifting her face when David introduced her. "This is Laura Corpin. But everyone calls her T.O." Her eyes were hazel, in a pool of perfectly white sclera. Tower reasoned she must be lacking in confidence as she constantly avoided direct eye contact and kept moving her hands behind her body.

"Hello. What's up, Mark?" Tower showed them to his office arrangement of three chairs circled in front of a large oak desk. Tower had it custom-made. Just behind the varnished wood, the desk was complete with a two-inch metal plate, covered with two layers of Kevlar, tough enough to stop most bullets.

Mark David started to sit. Corpin was still standing and angled closer to the door than a chair.

Tower moved the chair one foot in her direction. "Look, I don't know why you're here but I'm here to help. I've known Mark for a very long time. I trust him, and I think he would not bring you here unless he thought I could help."

She sat down.

"Here's the deal, Frank." Mark David took out a piece of paper. "T.O. filed a missing persons report two weeks ago. We've been working hard on the case, but nothing so far."

She interrupted him. The quiet one started to roar. "I want to hire you!"

"Okay..."

"The police aren't doing enough." There was a touch of anger in her eyes. "Except Mark, of course. But he's in another department."

"Our missing persons unit is not that big. They did their checks, but so far, there's nothing." Mark David looked down at his paper. "He's been missing almost two weeks, ever since the report was filed."

Tower took out his own sheet of paper. "If I can, let me ask a few questions. Who is missing?"

T.O. answered. "His name is Wakefield. Preston Wakefield. He was supposed to meet me for a quick bite, never showed, and at first, I didn't think anything about it. Then a couple of days later, I went by his place and found some old mail starting to pile up."

Tower was busy scribbling. "What about work? Mark?"

"This is information passed on to me. They got a call from him that he was sick. That was a Wednesday morning. On Thursday, they called him when he failed to show up. Got no response. Everything was going fine at work, he just got promoted. He didn't seem depressed, got along with co-workers, kept to himself."

"What about family? Wife? Siblings?" Tower took out a second sheet of paper.

"He always said he was estranged from his family." T.O. crossed her arms. "The police can only do so much. I need someone looking for him twenty-four-seven. That's you."

"Frank, she asked me if I knew any private investigators and I thought of you."

Tower posed a question. "You sure you don't want to give it a couple more days? See what police find?"

"They found nothing! I know he's in trouble. I don't want to wait more days. I need you, Frank Tower. Will you take the case?"

Tower shuffled his papers into a neat stack. "Okay. I'm on board. Mark, thanks for bringing her by. You can go. I'll get her home."

Mark David got up to leave. "If I hear anything, I'll pass it on to you both."

"Thanks. C'mon, we've got work to do."

David closed the door and was gone.

T.O. pressed her fingers into her forehead and rubbed. "I keep thinking, where could he be? We go way back. In sixth grade, he chipped a tooth when we were playing in the yard. Just play stuff. My mom got pretty mad. In high school, he pranked me into wearing men's clothes to go bowling." She sat back in the chair and smiled. The smile then turned into a ragged line. "I just have that feeling that he's in a bad place." On her right hand, Tower noticed a heart-shaped mole.

T.O. briefly looked outside and sighed, as if the world was moving on and leaving behind the memory of Preston Wakefield.

Tower asked, "If he grew up here, where's his family?"

"Just after high school, they moved away. Pres ran away three times, always returning to Stilton Bay. When he was eighteen, they couldn't touch him."

"And you haven't been in touch with his family?"

"No."

Tower picked up a briefcase and moved toward the door.

"Where are we going?"

"Stop by his place and his job. Check around."

"Thanks for taking this on. Pres, I call him Pres. He would have contacted me by now. I just want you to know. He's my best friend."

3

Their drive took them through the lifeline of Stilton Bay, Florida. The downtown business district. A summer sun glinted off the tables in front of Ray's Restaurant. Tower rolled down his window and took in the salty mixture of seaside air, suntan lotion, and just a hint of dried beer on the sidewalk. Stilton Bay was on the water and downtown gave tourists quick access to the beach.

When Tower stopped driving, he was almost a mile due south of downtown, all east of Interstate I-95. He assessed the location. Two building security cameras appeared to be broken. Each floor had its own laundry and dryer. Stairs on the north and south sides of the building. A parking lot took up the entire front of the place. There was no view of the ocean, just a perfect angle of the sides of three taller condos. The place looked old and the peeling paint in some areas did not help the overall condition of the complex.

"You have a key?" Tower watched T.O. pull the key from her purse.

"This guy has been locked out three times. The first one, they forgive you. After that, they charge you sixty-five bucks each time. So, yes, I have a key. I was backup."

She opened the door. "The police have already been here." Tower motioned for her to stay back, let him inside first.

He did a fast sweep of the apartment. One small area for TV watching, next to a galley-style kitchen. On the other side, a hallway led to a moderate-sized master bedroom. Another bedroom was at the end of the hallway. Inside that room, Tower found a desk and no computer. He backed all the way out to the front door.

"You see anything missing?" Tower asked.

"Police asked the same thing." She looked around as she answered. "Naw, don't see anything out of place."

"Okay. Stay there a bit more."

Tower again made his way through the apartment. He snapped on plastic gloves. He saw four rings of residue on the glass table. "Was Preston a beer drinker?"

"Not really."

Tower looked in the fridge. A half-empty bottle of apple juice was pushed to the back. The rest was the usual: a partial head of lettuce, a plastic bin full of tomatoes, three different kinds of ketchup, two slices of pizza in a baggie, and a large raw chicken ready for roasting.

No beer.

Tower checked the small kitchen garbage bin. He still could not find any bottles. Next came the search of the office. T.O. showed him where a laptop computer was missing. She explained police took that with them. The room was immaculate. On the wall were photographs of Preston with T.O. and others on hiking trails. In another, they were riding bicycles. Pictures of Preston at the beach in Stilton Bay and at a restaurant. Maybe Ray's place.

In the photograph T.O. was smiling. She had long hair layered against her back. The nails were short and trimmed. No polish. Preston looked business-like. His shoes were moderate, not pricy, the shirt was flannel, and he had a regular build, not stocky. T.O. stared at Tower for a long time.

"Are you married?"

The question.

The one single, without-a-doubt, don't-want-to-touch-it area of his life, and she opened the door.

Tower said, "Yeah, I'm married. She's with her sister for a couple of weeks."

She gave him a look Tower tried to brush off. According to the paper-work Tower filled out, T.O. was just twenty-two. Tower was thirty-eight. While working a case years earlier, a question just like that from a client led to other personal inquiries and an affair. A moment that almost led to the break-up of his marriage. Two years of pleading and hard relationship work moved the marriage back into the happy range. Anytime he heard that question, Tower started putting up walls.

"I miss her," he said. "Her name is Shannon."

He kept up his search.

Tower pulled out drawers. He could see where police shuffled every-thing. "Where did Preston like to go? Any clubs? There aren't that many in Stilton Bay. Ya have to go over to Fort Lauderdale or, better yet, Miami."

She crossed and uncrossed her arms. "We would sometimes get a bottle of wine and go down to the beach. They don't like you to drink down there, but we go kinda late." She stared at his photograph. "Preston was married once. He was very young and didn't know what he was getting into. She left him for someone else. I helped him through that. Another reason for those long talks on the beach."

"You have any recent text messages, emails, voicemails?"

She handed him her cell phone. "Just that he had a meeting a couple of days before he went missing. Don't know where or why, but I think it was important."

"How so?"

"He mentioned it four times. Once or twice is a lot for Pres, but four times, I don't know."

Tower scrolled down through the listing of texts. "He had no pets?"

"Complex doesn't allow pets. He wanted a dog."

"Where's Preston's car?"

"Downstairs. The keys were on his dresser."

Tower sat down in a large chair. "If he met someone here, there was no struggle. He might have gone with them. To me, it means he knew the person."

She stood in front of the wall of photographs. "There's one missing."

Tower joined her. "Which one?"

"There was a photograph of the both of us standing on the beach in Key Biscayne. It was his favorite."

"What about his phone?"

"Police took it. They say they found it here in the apartment."

Tower's thoughts converged into a theory that he did not want to share with anyone just yet. He imagined himself as Preston, coming to the door, letting in a familiar face, talking, and then being subdued somehow and taken away. All that happened and yet no one heard anything. For the moment, Tower ruled out a woman or at least one small in stature. Unless he was lured out of the apartment, without keys and cell phone, the attacker would have to let him lean on him, take Preston out as if he was under the influence of drink.

Tower spent more than fifteen minutes photographing everything in the apartment. He snapped pics of the circular rings on the table and the inside of the fridge.

There was still time to take what a killer would call trophies like the missing picture from the wall. A computer and other items left behind. The photograph, Tower thought, was personal. His cell phone rang.

"Frank. It's Mark. We have something. Meet us here. If you have her, bring her along, but keep her at a distance."

Tower pushed the phone close to his face. "Where am I going?"

"T-Town."

4

T-Town was the bruised side of Stilton Bay. All of the Avenues started with the letter T, running north and south. The entire area was just west of I-95 in South Florida. Fences in yards were in need of a few planks, like missing teeth. Some homes were boarded up after years of owners unable to do repairs and watching them decay through lay-offs and late payments.

Tower's destination was Denton Park, which remained the oldest one in the city. City leaders on three occasions put more money into the park, adding a new surface to the basketball court, meeting rooms and a computer lab. Two people were hired to run the complex.

T.O. said nothing as they drove.

Tower pulled up next to an unmarked detective SUV. A fire rescue truck was pulling away, no lights on. Tower made her stay in the car for a minute. He walked up to the yellow crime tape line and stood. A canopy was set up over a park bench. Detective Mark David was walking around the tent. A female detective Tower did not recognize stood taking notes.

He saw the victim.

Tower recognized him from the photographs. What stood out were his eyes. They were open, wider than normal. Since the body before him did not go with fire rescue, Tower knew this had changed into a suspicious death scene. Maybe more. The bench was set up to overlook a pond. Two ducks glided by, oblivious to the death just a few yards away. Tower noticed the deceased's head was angled in an odd way. The hands were placed on his lap.

For a moment Tower thought about what people always said, asking why police let the body sit out there like that, without covering them up. Tower knew it was the same reason some crime techs moved in the manner they did. They worked from the outside in. The reason was to make sure they didn't step on any evidence. After the body was declared dead, they could back up and process the scene in a giant circle, always moving inward toward the body. By covering up the body, key evidence could be lost, the reason why the public was kept back so much. Police, detectives, and crime techs needed room to slowly process, photograph, and log each element. Some crime scenes could take days to finish.

Tower cringed at the thought of TV detectives walking up to a pivotal piece of evidence and picking it up, sometimes with their bare hands. It just wasn't done that way. A marker might be placed near the evidence, then photographed from several angles and bagged and tagged before being touched.

"Maybe bringing her here was a bad idea." Mark David caught Tower by surprise.

"He was posed?" Tower kept looking at the victim.

"You know I can't tell you any of that." Mark David looked over at the scene by the pond, then back to Tower.

Tower took in a deep chest full of sun-cooked Florida air. "I think he was posed. His eyes are open way too wide. I don't see any blood around, so he was moved here. The surveillance cameras haven't worked in this park for years. Someone buttoned up his shirt, so there might be something hidden once you get him to the morgue. And just what is he looking at?"

Mark David gave a half-smile and just as quickly turned serious. "We're still going through this. We need an identification but that can wait till we get him back to the lab. We've sent for dental records. We'll arrange for T.O. to look at him there at the morgue."

They both turned in the direction of the loud scream just left of Tower. T.O. was standing in the street, hands on her head, yelling at the long stack of clouds.

Tower ran to her. "It's him," she yelled. "It's Pres. What are they doing to him?"

He hugged her and pulled T.O. toward his car, all in one motion. She started to cry, then stopped. "I promised myself no tears."

"It's okay to let it out."

"He looked like he was trying to tell me something." T.O. looked out the window.

"They might ask you to identify him later. You okay with that?"

She nodded. "I want to change our arrangement." T.O. pulled her attention from the scene and her eyes bored into Tower. "Now I want to hire you to find out what happened to him and why."

"That's a job for the police. I can't get in their way."

"You're Frank Tower. I heard about you. I know you can find out things the police can't."

"If they think I'm in their way, they can mess with my license."

Tower was still, watching the techs work. Call it a cop's instinct. There were moments when he was on the force when Tower knew something was about to happen. In those moments, the perceptions he got saved his life several times. Scientists called it gaze detection.

He had it now. The sense that someone was watching him. Tower told T.O. to stay by the car. It wouldn't be that far off for a killer to visit a scene. He could take it all in, sucking up the negative energy, making himself believe the location of his body-dump gave him strength. Tower checked his Glock and stared at the rows of trees just behind him. The sensation was unmistakable. He sensed it, he knew it. They were being watched.

A tree branch popped back up into its original position. Tower was now running, fast as a thirty-something ex-cop could run. When he reached the tree, he caught just a flashing glimpse of a car taking off down a side street. The vehicle was gone before he could even get a color, let alone a tag number. Without surveillance cameras nearby, hopes of finding the car were bleak. He returned to his car and put the memory away.

5

"Pres gave me the nickname T.O." She took a small sip from a soda and pushed the glass away like it was the last thing she wanted in life. "He said I was so feisty and out of control, he told me to take a time out. He said it so much he just gave me the nickname, T.O. for time out." Her bottom lip trembled. "I miss him. This is going to hurt."

They were sitting outside at the corner table at Ray's Restaurant, just yards from a row of bottlebrush trees. Late afternoon on a Monday, and for Tower, it was as if a week were packed into one day.

"Again, Preston have any family here?" Tower stuck the last French fry into his mouth, leaving a clean plate.

"Naw, just me. And I'm not family. His parents are gone and we just had each other."

"Thought maybe you two might…"

"With Pres? No. After his first marriage turned to shit, he backed off that conversation. We were just close friends." She took the glass and tossed the contents into the grass. The glass came down hard on the table.

Tower said, "You're looking for a place to direct your anger. And possibly some blame, but don't put it on yourself. Someone did this to him. It has nothing to do with you."

"I know."

"We got some other flavors out there, if that's not what you want." The words came from the owner, Ray Lane. Stout and with caramel-toned skin, Lane always met customers with a full smile. His place was the most popular in Stilton Bay.

Tower shook his hand. "What's up, Ray."

"I'm happier than a minnow in shallow water." Lane and Tower laughed. T.O. stayed somber. Her sorrow flattened Lane's smile. "I heard about what happened. Sorry you lost your friend."

T.O. managed a grin with water-rimmed eyes.

"Thanks for everything, Ray. And I don't mean just today."

"How is your mother?" He picked up the plate and empty glasses.

Tower shook his head. "You mean Jackie? We're headed that way. I still owe you, Ray."

"Don't owe me anything. See you next time."

Tower could see the curiosity building up in T.O. Next came the questions.

"Why don't you call her your mother?" she asked.

"We are headed to her place. It's a rehab center. Just one stop before I take you home."

Several minutes into the drive, her voice had an edge. "You never answered my question."

"There was a time when Jackie loved drugs more than me. She would leave me at home, alone. I was about four years old. She hit T-Town for, at that time, crack. She moved on to other things later. Got so hungry one time, I got the front door open and went searching for food and water. My pants were dirty from two days' wear, I needed a bath. You could probably smell me from ten yards away. I could have been snatched up and killed by some maniac. But I ran into Ray. He found me. Took me in, got me fed. His wife cleaned me up. I had a new friend. Man saved my life on too many occasions."

"And Jackie?"

"Took three years, two arrests for burglary, but she finally got cleaned up herself. Convinced some backers to help her open up a rehab and she's been there ever since."

"And she's not Mom?"

"She hasn't been Mom since I was born. Jackie is just fine."

A used, discarded condom on the sidewalk served as a landmark for the Never Too Late Drug Rehabilitation Center. A large square of once-upon-a-time grass gave up its fight for life years ago. Now, tall, stringy weeds dotted the front. Large all-glass doors were the only semblance of security as there were no cameras. The front desk clerk could at least see trouble coming up the walkway through those glass doors.

Jackie made her way to the parking lot where Tower parked. Her face was a spiderweb pattern of brown wrinkles stretching into her stark white hair. Tower once told her each wrinkle had its own story to tell. She was thin, drug-addicted thin, even though the word clean had been with her for a few years. The only sparkle came from her eyes as Tower closed the car door.

"My Frankie!" She started to approach for a hug, hesitated, then backed up and wrapped her arms around her own frail frame.

"Been quiet? Like to ask you about something." Tower looked over the place.

"No hello? Nothing? C'mon, Frankie, you can give your mother a..."

"We had a murder up at the park. The road to the park runs right past here. You see anything, hear anything last night?"

She stroked her chin. "Can't say. No, not really." She turned to T.O. "Who is this?"

"Meet T.O. I'm helping her with something."

Tower scanned the place with a cop's vision. He wanted to look into cars and speak with a few people. That, he figured, would have to wait for another day.

"I need a favor. You don't get a lot of folks coming down this end of town. This is a perfect spot to hide, or better, hide something. If you see anything, please give me a call."

"No problem, Frankie. You want to come inside for a minute?"

Memories poured down on him like Florida raindrops. If there was any amount of patience coming from her now, where was it when he was a tyke and needed the basics? He thought about the missed birthday parties because the money was spent on drugs rather than presents. An avalanche of nightmare days and nights stacked up like one giant demon called abuse. Maybe there would be a day when he could even speak the word forgiveness. Just not today.

"We've got to go."

Tower directed T.O. to get back into the car. Once they were past two prostitutes on Tandon Avenue, he spoke. "Too much happened when I was a kid."

Tower crossed back over, eastbound, under I-95 to the gleaming side of Stilton Bay, headed for T.O.'s apartment. There was an uptick in cool air. A yellow tinge of evening sunlight covered everything in a warm hue. Sunset was less than thirty minutes away. Before he could park, Tower answered his cell phone.

"Frank, it's Mark. Where are you?"

"About to drop off T.O. Why?"

"Come to the morgue right now. Bring her with you. She can do an identification."

"Something you're not telling me."

"Frank, you have to see this."

6

Stilton Bay maintained its own morgue, very close to the police station. Run by Elly Kent, the place was awash in white, from the tiles on the floor to the walls and baseboards.

Detective Mark David was waiting for them as they entered the lobby.

"T.O., thanks for coming in. If you'll come with me, I'll take you to an observation room. Are you up to doing this?"

"Yes. But I want Frank with me."

"That's not..." David was silent for a moment. "It's okay. This way."

He escorted them down the hall, past a security checkpoint, past three sets of double doors, and into a pre-observation room. The temperature was noticeably cooler. The smell of chemicals and death permeated the air. Before them was a window with a dark green curtain.

Mark David stood next to T.O. "You ready?"

She nodded. Reluctantly. The curtain moved.

T.O. stood rigid. Finally, she whispered, "That's him. That's Preston."

For Tower, death in this final form was always surreal. Rigor made the body so stiff, to the point facial features were wooden. No matter the background, skin tones were off. On numerous occasions, Tower, coming home as a teen, expected to see Jackie this same way. He thought the drugs would one day claim her body and he'd open the door to a stone-hard resemblance of the woman who birthed him. She managed to survive.

When T.O. moved back from the window, Tower moved closer. He examined what he could since the body was covered in a white sheet. Preston's eyes were now closed, and the holes from the stitches to keep them open were clearly visible. There were scrapes on his face from some type of physical trauma or a fall.

"T.O., thank you. Someone will accompany you to the lobby. You can wait there."

She looked at Tower, then followed an officer.

"I need you to see something." Mark David's voice sounded like cop-speak. Official, not social. Tower went with him into a room with three other people and found an empty chair.

"Frank, you know some of the people in this room. There's Sania Powell, James Corker, and Jake May. My homicide unit. I want you to know everyone is against me showing you this. Don't mind telling you Jake was the most vocal."

"It breaks the chain." Jake May was around six-four, observed strict eating habits, and from Tower's past experience on the force, was dependable and loyal to the badge. "If this goes to court, we could have problems. Breaking the chain of evidence. I still say it's a bad idea."

Tower looked confused.

Mark David opened a laptop. "You were a cop, Frank. We shouldn't be showing you this. I okayed it. They all disagreed. Civilians don't get to see these things. But I thought you should know."

Mark David put on gloves and held up an evidence bag. Inside the bag was a thumb drive. "What I'm about to tell you has to be kept in confidence. And I'll only tell you so much. The reason for all this will be evident in a minute. Do I have your agreement on this?"

Tower's slow answer brought on quiet jeers from the three in the room. Sania slapped the side of her pants, brushing against her Glock. "He can't be trusted. Get'm outta here and let's get back to the case."

"I agree." Tower stared at the laptop.

May turned his back on all of them. "He doesn't even know what he's agreeing to. I don't like it."

"I'm not going to jam up your investigation." Tower's voice had a finality to it and the room got quiet.

May pulled out a tape recorder, started the thing in record mode, and put it on the table. He spoke a tad louder. "This is being recorded on Monday evening." May mentioned everyone who was in the room, then yielded to Mark David.

"Frank, this thumb drive was taken from the body of Preston Wakefield during an autopsy. The drive was pulled from the heart of Mr. Wakefield by medical examiner Elly Kent. Mr. Tower, have you ever seen this before?"

"No."

"I'm pulling the thumb drive out of the evidence bag and we are putting it into a city-owned laptop."

The blank screen showed one folder. Once Mark David clicked on the folder, Tower looked at the screen and swallowed hard.

On the screen, the group saw:

MAKE SURE FRANK TOWER SEES ALL OF YOUR NOTES

I WILL KNOW

"I ask you, Frank Tower, do you recognize any of this?" Mark David waited.

Tower started to shake his head, then remembered he had to answer verbally. "No, I have not seen any of this before."

Mark David opened the file.

In his five years on the force and another five as a P.I., many things had shocked him. There were so many creative ways suspects used to store bodies, it always amazed Tower. In some cases, the brutality of the injuries stunned him. What Tower saw next was simple yet shook him to the bone.

There, on the screen, was a clock. And the clock was counting down. Right at the moment, one day, seventeen hours, and forty-nine seconds. Now forty-eight. Forty-seven.

Mark David was to the point. "Do you know why this killer or killers wanted to single you out?"

"No." Tower felt a drop of sweat move down a crease in his forehead and slide toward his left eye. He pointed a finger at the laptop screen. "I just know that's how much time we have left before he makes his next kill."

7

T.O. waited in the car. Tower met with a restless Mark David. "Frank, I need you to look through your P.I. files. Think, who would you piss off enough to do this?"

"The list would stretch to Tallahassee. I've investigated hundreds of people. Husband cheats, work comp cheats, you name it." Tower kicked at a rock in the road. "We don't have much time, I get it. I'll stay up all night. Just let me go through my files."

"Thanks."

"Mark, how did Preston die?"

"You know I can't tell you that. It's an open case."

Tower was ready to read Mark's reaction. "I saw the body. He looked like his lips might have been sewn shut. If the killer did that to his nose, he could then just watch him die. I saw some trauma around the nose."

"You know I can't confirm any of that."

"I don't think this is all aimed at me. Something much larger is happening. I just don't know what yet."

Instead of going home, T.O. wanted to be left with a former college roommate. Tower went straight to his office. There he had a day bed for sleep. His main focus was on who could be targeting him with a countdown clock.

He pulled out boxes of old cases, going all the way back to when he opened his P.I. office. After an hour of searching through files, refiring old memories, Tower came up with a very short list of four names. One name in particular was a defendant he tried to help, spending seven weeks aiding the defense team. A jury still found him guilty. Tower crossed off the name, as a quick check showed he was still in prison. In another case, a woman vowed to get back at Tower for exposing a get-rich scheme. Another check proved she was living three states away. The search left him with two names, which he would forward to Mark David.

Before he went to sleep, Tower called his wife Shannon. The conversation was long, running an hour, and when he shut down his cell phone, it was close to midnight.

Tower could not sleep.

All he thought about was the clock moving toward zero.

8

A burnt-orange orb pushed up out of the Atlantic, capping the incoming waves in crimson. Fingers of foam stretched out of the cobalt sea and stayed onshore for several seconds, as if holding on until they were absorbed by the sandy beach. The air carried a strong musk of suntan lotion and brine. Just to the south, fishing boats were packed with tourists. Ship captains were helping fishermen scoop bait fish from the ocean. Goggle eye and pilchards were caught and dumped into the bins, ready to be used to catch mahi-mahi and amberjack. The Tuesday sun blanched Stilton Bay and areas west, all the way to the property of Saneele Gunson. She was up with the first brush of a morning breeze, clippers in hand, snipping and cutting her Ixora bush.

Gunson's house was on the far western edge of the city, even farther west than T-Town. She enjoyed her separation from everyone and everything. Her neighbors were an occasional iguana, an avalanche of lizards, opossum, and raccoons. A canal marked the end of her property, and she stayed away from the bank at night because of alligators. Her six cats also knew the drill and only roamed close to the house.

Her alarm clock was the blue jays and grackles. The birds chirped their messages and were the only sounds she heard during her morning jaunts.

In mid-clip of a plant, she thought there was the clear snap of a branch not more than fifteen yards from her. Gunson stopped moving and listened. Her place was like a forest, thanks to her decision to plant trees by the dozens. Her driveway was dedicated to rows of Crape Myrtle trees. Behind them, there were rows of Rose apple and the patchy brown bark of a few gumbo limbos.

She crafted pathways through her private garden. Still, the sun managed to send spears of light through the dipping branches, leaving her face dappled in shadow circles.

There was another snap of a branch.

Saneele looked down the path and saw nothing. She held the clippers at an angle, like a weapon. Her handgun, a small caliber Colt she'd had since retiring seven years ago, was stuffed in a kitchen drawer. Fifty-plus yards away.

The birds stopped chirping.

Her gaze whipped around in quick movements, left to right, hoping to see anyone crossing one of her paths.

Nothing.

A soft pat of her empty jeans pocket let her know she'd left her cell phone on a counter. She was alone with just the protection of her tall trees and the clippers. Then, for a millisecond, Saneele thought she caught sight of a person making his way toward her location. The intruder's gait was quiet and careful.

She weighed her options. Persistent right leg soreness meant running was out. The canal was a possibility, even with the knowledge of patrolling gators. This was June. Mating season for alligators and they were on the move. She took the clippers, held them out in front of her, and took several steps to another tree, all in hopes of reaching the house.

This could be an overreaction. Just simply walk up to him, offer a friendly word, and see what he wanted. A wayward stranger might need help or directions. A misunderstanding could explain the near-silent entry into her plant world.

Then she saw all of him.

Something was covering his face and a contraption was strapped to his chest. Her earlier fears were confirmed.

Now, just get away.

Run.

Saneele made it to a southern maple. She stayed there, planted against the tree trunk, waiting for any sounds of being tracked. There were none. Armed with just a modicum of confidence, she focused on a live oak and scampered fifteen feet to another tree trunk. She leaned against the hard bark and waited. All she could think about was keeping her breathing down. Her blouse rose and fell with the rapidity of a baby bird. Saneele's heart thundered in her chest. Fear was winning.

She saw the man again.

A figure in the shape of a charcoal-colored nightmare angled a direct path in her direction and stopped. She looked for a weapon in his hands. Maybe she should just yell for help. Instead, she stayed quiet, rather than give up her exact position.

The nearest neighbor was too far away. All her well-planned seclusion was now haunting her. When she looked for the figure again, he was gone. Then, three clear, distinct footsteps broke the dense morning air like cuts on the skin. And they were getting closer.

Saneele reasoned it was now clear. Either stay right there and fight or run to the canal and swim to the other side. Fighting was not on her top list of accomplishments in life. She pushed the clippers into her jeans. And ran as best she could.

She tried to increase her speed. Her movements were a jerky collection of seldom used muscles and flailing arms. Her purpose was surprise. If she could catch the figure off guard, she could get a big enough jump to give her time to get to safety.

She devised a new goal. Her gardener's shack.

There was no phone in the tiny place, yet once inside, she could lock the door and hide behind several bags of mulch. The shack also had the cover of years of plant growth. All the wooden boards had a skin of passion plants. A steady air raid of butterflies dipped in and around the blossoms. Saneele got quiet. She looked down and saw her right hand was trembling almost to the point of being uncontrollable. Her entire body ached. In the roasted June air, lines of sweat streamed down her face onto her chest. She was two trees away from the door of the shack. Another two minutes of quiet gave her a signal to move a few feet. After checking the grounds, she darted the short distance to the next tree.

The sounds of faded footsteps made her freeze.

The steps were far enough away that it was impossible to determine how close he was to her. For Saneele, nothing mattered until she got inside the shack. One more tree to go. She waited three more minutes and made her move. Once there, she grabbed the tree like an old friend. Saneele tried to repress her breathing. The hard pants kept coming. Controlled breathing was next. Just like a mother in labor, she kept up the low, even hiss of exhales. Calmness returned. The shack was just feet away.

Just get inside.

Saneele took two, then three quiet steps toward the door. She was almost there. Three more. Two more steps. The door was in sight. She looked up at the small window in the doorframe.

Saneele stopped.

All the air burst from her lungs like a blown tire. She was shaking with such intensity, it was all she could do to avoid blacking out. Her eyes were fixed on the miniature window.

The figure was already inside the shack.

He was staring at her like a predator sizing up the last steps before making a strike. She turned and ran. The canal was her only choice.

Seconds into her run to the canal, she heard the heavy steps coming after her. Just enough of a jump to give her a slight chance to reach the water first. She ran past her prized blooming magnolia trees, under a black olive and the spreading branches of a traveler's helper. The footsteps behind her were louder now, no longer concealed. The canal was less than twenty feet away. When she reached the bank, Saneele looked into the water. No snakes or gators. She gripped the grass on the bank and eased herself into the dark-green water as quietly as possible. The deeper water was yet another fifteen feet.

On her right, she spotted a creature. An alligator.

Just eyes above the water, the gator was moving toward her, all the time picking up speed. The alligator was close enough for her to see the menacing eyes and just the top of its green-black back. Saneele was splashing now. Her arms thrashed at the water to get moving, away from the gator, away from the intruder, away from everything. The gator was closing in and within seconds she would have to fight him off.

Something grabbed her foot.

She kicked hard but nothing could pry her foot from the grip. Saneele felt herself being pulled backward. All her efforts did not matter; she was moving back toward the bank.

Almost as if in one swift motion, she was hauled up on the bank in a heap of heavy breathing and soaked clothes.

A foot pressed down on her chest and she could not move.

The sun prevented her from seeing his face. She squinted a few times to block the glare of direct sunlight. Her focus was off from the canal water in her eyes.

Then she saw him standing over her.

A heavy mechanical voice sounded like something out of a movie.

"You are mine."

9

Tower cleared all his current cases, telling clients he would resume the work in a few days. He put all of his effort into Preston Wakefield and the message.

He spent two hours on the phone with Shannon. Half the conversation was convincing her to stay and not come home.

Tower phoned T.O. to check on her. She decided to stay with her friend and not go to work. While there, plans were started for a small memorial service for Preston.

Tower thought about the physical appearance of Preston in the morgue. He was positive Preston's lips were, at one time, sewn together. There were also punch holes on the nose. Tower envisioned the killer made sure Preston couldn't breathe, then stood by and watched him die.

The thought consumed Tower. There were so many factors that made up a killer; so many, in fact, that psychologists and others had spent more than a hundred years trying to come up with the reasoning on why they kill.

Tower got almost no sleep. A shower would have to come later. In a process that started the previous evening, he did a full background check on Preston. He found no arrests, no liens or major outstanding debt. A check of county records showed he received three moving violations over a three-year period. He liked to drive fast. He had no bankruptcy and no evictions. What Tower could not find was any connection whatsoever to himself. He never saw Preston Wakefield until he found him behind police crime tape, on a bench with his eyes sewn open.

Everything led Tower back to the same question of why he was included in the computer file message. The killer obviously wanted him to know every move he was making.

Tower got in his car and drove.

An unshaven, somewhat stinky Frank Tower slid behind the counter at Ray's Restaurant and ordered three scrambled eggs, two waffles, a strip of bacon, and two cups of coffee. Black.

"Not going to ask you how ya doing." Ray emerged from the kitchen wearing a cook's apron streaked with two distinct lines of grease. "Frank, you look like oven-roasted roadkill."

"Don't get too close." Tower waved him off. "I need a shower."

Ray waved his arms, as if he was pushing the sausage and egg aroma in Tower's direction. "Let me cover you with my breakfast smell. Don't get any better than this." He gave that familiar Ray laugh, the one Tower first heard as a tyke. The same laugh that taught Tower there was a life after a mother abandoned you for street chemicals. Early on, Ray was Tower's lifeline, and with no man in the house, the closest thing he had to a father.

Tower left a big tip. Before leaving the place and almost bumping into the restaurant clean-up man, he had a question for Ray.

"Forgot to ask you last time. Preston Wakefield. Did he ever stop in here?"

Ray's normally bulbous cheeks flattened. The smile was gone. "Yeah, he did. The police never asked me about it yet."

"Was he in here recently?"

"Yes. Just a couple of days before..."

"I get it." Tower came back to the counter and lowered his voice so the conversation was just between the two of them. "Was he meeting with anyone?"

"No, not that I recall."

Tower looked around the place. No surveillance cameras.

"No cameras in here?"

Ray's smile was back. "No. Made my customers nervous. Took'm out."

"Thanks, Ray."

Tower thought about heading home for a few minutes to clean up. At the top of his list was a talk at Preston's workplace. His cell phone hummed.

"Frank?"

"Yeah..."

Tower recognized Mark David's voice. "We're letting you know only because we're putting out a press release. It's a silver alert. We have a missing person."

10

Tower drove to Saneele Gunson's home and parked. Before him, two police units were in the circular driveway. In Florida, a silver alert was for any elderly person who might have wandered off and was now missing. Seven other cars were parked all along the street leading up to the house. Tower saw people all over the property in search mode, looking for her.

Mark David's unmarked SUV was also near the front walkway. Tower was now driving his van. The extended cab van was built by Tower for surveillance missions. He also had a small desk and lamp set up with a laptop. For several minutes Tower was checking on the background of one Saneele Wanda Gunson, married twice, one child who died years earlier, one husband deceased, four jobs, including research assistant at two universities. She retired in Stilton Bay almost seven years ago. After her husband passed, Tower surmised she amassed enough money to buy the eight acres of land with an untold number of trees.

Tower closed up his van and walked to the front gate of the house. He followed the same routine: make yourself very visible, then wait until Mark David has time to approach you. Sixteen minutes into his wait, David motioned him away from the small crowd of people.

"What are you allowed to tell me, Mark?" Tower pulled out a small pad.

"Not much. I'll tell you what I told the media. Nothing else. We've got a sixty-eight-year-old woman who is missing. You already know her name. Between us, we made a decision to warn the public. In Preston Wakefield's death, we think the killer or killers are still out there and dangerous. We're already getting calls about whether the two are related. I can't share any of that with you. Still, she's been missing since people showed up and she was supposed to host a luncheon about planting. Her friends arrived, looked around, and didn't find her. We found her clippers by the canal bank."

Tower was still writing. "You have divers out?"

"Yeah, got a team of them. We have two sharpshooters on the bank. That's customary when you have alligators nearby. So far, nothing."

"If there was some type of struggle, I'm sure you couldn't tell me that, but I have to ask, have you been inside the house?"

Mark David's face turned to the Gunson home, then back to Tower. "Why do you ask?"

"Okay, Mark, here goes. I took a look at Preston Wakefield's apartment. On the coffee table, there appeared to be water rings, like from a beer can. Preston did not drink beer or any sodas. A photograph of the victim and T.O. was missing from the apartment. Inside her home, you might want to check for beer rings or if the killer took something. That is, if she was taken."

"Thank you." Mark David turned to leave, then spoke over his shoulder. "Sorry ahead of time if I find something that I can't share with you."

"Understood."

Tower watched the detective move inside the house.

Forty minutes later, Mark David came out. He looked once at Tower, then walked to his unmarked and drove off. Two other unmarked police units followed him. David's look was somber.

Tower knew what must have happened. If he found the water rings on a table, then this was no longer a matter of someone simply walking off. This had to be because the clock was winding down and another victim was in the hands of a killer.

11

"Thank you for letting me on your property." Frank Tower put on a hat. The noon sun was unyielding.

Rockland Canter pointed to a beatdown Chevy pickup truck with three dents on the side. The truck's color was now reduced to a blend of faded red and road dust. The floorboard, the seats, dash, everything was layered in the heavy dust of the unattended grazing land of Canter's property.

"I just use this side for a few cattle and one bull. Never come over here much."

"You ever going to sell?" Tower kept the conversation light and away from the object of his attention.

"Had another six offers last week. They want to put up houses. Not much free land like mine." Everyone called him Rock. His twenty-seven acres represented the last big parcel of open land in Broward County. The value jumped each year.

They stopped at the southern end of the property and got out. Tower took out his binoculars. "Talk to her much?"

"Sany? Naw. Hardly at all." Rock looked like he was surveying a place to spit. "We keep our space."

Tower stood on the bank and looked across the deep green canal water. He was able to see her house and the police investigation.

"Sorry to hear she's missing." Rock wiped his mouth of the remaining spittle.

"Can you identify anyone over there?" Tower handed the binocs to Rock.

He held them to his face and moved his view left to right. "Sure. Well, maybe not. I thought I remembered the names and faces. Now, I'm not so sure. But I know her." He pointed to his right.

With his naked eye, Tower spotted a tall woman. She had the same skin tone as Ray. "Yeah, I know her. Shit, she probably knows every person in this town."

Tower knew her as well. Janine Iwan. Social worker. When he got the binoculars back, Tower watched her motioning with her hands, talking to friends, pointing to the place where, Tower guessed, the clippers were found. Iwan looked worried. She never stayed in one position, just kept moving around, pointing and talking, as if that might make Saneele reappear. Tower watched as a police diver rose out of the depths of the canal. He was being watched closely by two armed Stilton Bay officers. All eyes were on the water. There were no alligators in sight; still, they had to be on the watch.

Tower checked his watch. If indeed she was taken, the detectives had just scant hours to find Saneele Gunson before the clock deadline. Tower stepped back to the rust-marked Chevy and opened his laptop. He continued more research on Gunson. Several minutes into his search, he could not find any connection between himself, Preston, or the missing woman. The ages between them were so drastically different. There was nothing in common.

He turned his attention back to the house where another crime tech team had arrived. Tower was able to see into the house and discovered one crime tech taking pictures of the kitchen table and other areas. Gunson had large windows, probably to enjoy the landscape she so carefully planted. He was about to check everything from another angle when his phone hummed.

"Tower..."

"You Tower?" His voice was business-like, as if the man was careful about his words.

"Can I help you?"

"Well, this woman, she, ah, well, she…"

"You've reached Frank Tower. Speak up. What woman?"

"She dropped your business card. And she, ah…"

There was a tinge of impatience in Tower's voice. "What woman?"

"I'm at the Sunset Bar and T.O. is causing a problem. I don't want to call the police."

"What is she doing?"

"She got into a locked part of the bar, and she's been drinking."

"And…"

"Well, Mr. Tower, she got into our expensive stuff, drinking, then throwing the glass against a wall. We can hear her, but we can't get inside."

"I'll be right there."

Tower was given a ride back to his van and he was in front of the bar fifteen minutes later. The owner just waved Tower toward the rear of the place and a storage area. Tower tried and the door was locked. Then he heard the crashing sound of glass on something hard.

"T.O., it's Frank. Let me in."

For three minutes, there was quiet. Then another crash. Tower yelled, "T.O., they're going to call the police, and right now, the police are busy trying to find who killed Preston. Do you want to interrupt all that? Open the door right now. I can have it busted down and they will make you pay for a new one."

There was a quiet click at the door. Tower entered the room. He didn't see T.O. One wall was awash in booze. There was smashed glass everywhere. The owner moved in behind the bar and waited. Tower kept looking around the room. There were walls of liquor, cases of beer, all stacked and ready for consumption. And in T.O.'s case, ready to be smeared on the wall. Tower walked cautiously, stepping over jagged shards, looking for her.

"T.O., I know what's going on. We're doing everything we can, but this is not the way to remember your friend. Where are you?"

He kept moving through the room. First, he saw a bottle of Jack Daniels on the floor. Six empty glasses were lined up, all waiting to be filled. T.O. was next to the bottle, head down, legs sprawled, with a view of the mess she created on the wall.

Tower sat down next to her. "I'm here to listen, not to judge. I've lost good friends too. As Preston might say, time out."

Her head tilted down even lower. Tower moved the glasses away from her. She spoke to the floor. "He doesn't have anyone for the funeral. Just me."

"When you arrange something, I'll be there. I promise."

Her hair was matted in areas, one fingernail was chipped. Tower noticed she was wearing the same clothes as the day before. Her jeans were laced with floor dust and she had a small cut on two fingers, probably from all the loose glass shards. Her eyes were dry. She kept the vow she made not to cry. A small smudge was over her left eyebrow.

Her head lifted only slightly. "I heard there's another person missing."

"We're not entirely sure..."

Her pain was evident. A new wrinkle had appeared in her left cheek. All of her words came out slow, as if it hurt to speak. Tufts of hair stuck out, never put back in place. Everything about T.O. spelled "leave me alone or I'll fuck you up."

She reached for another glass. "Not entirely sure. That's the kind of talk I heard when Pres was missing. Excuses."

Tower reached out and held her hand before the glass was in her grip. "I just left that house. The entire police department is on this. They're not big, but they are working it twenty-four-seven."

"I haven't had a drink." She paused. Clearly terrible thoughts were swirling through her, demons back from the depths of her memory bank. She stared blankly at the far wall like she was seeing ghost shadows. "My father used to drink. I did too, then I gave it up. Until this morning. I got mad. I didn't mean to do anything. I grabbed a key, sneaked in here, and first it was just one glass. Then two. And four more. I was out of control."

"I've had bad days myself. Mostly because of my...Jackie."

"You almost said mother." T.O. finally leaned her head back. "Pres was my designated savior."

Tower waited patiently for her to explain.

"You see, I used to get drunk a lot. Rum and a chaser, vodka, you put a brand name on it and I would drink it. Work and drink. Work and drink. And you know what? I never got arrested. Ya know why? Cause Pres would show up at some point and save my ass from going to jail. One night I was drinking so much, I told everyone I wouldn't stop. Preston came in, saw me drinking, and took the glass from my hand. Then, he threw that glass against the wall. Never touched a drop since. Until today. Yep. I called him my designated savior. And now, he's gone."

"I'm going to help you up. We'll get you cleaned up and work out a plan to repay the owner. Is that okay?"

"I guess so." Her voice was low and hard to hear. "I was throwing a glass in honor of Preston."

Tower smiled. "Well, maybe more than one glass." Tower got her standing and she immediately fell back down. T.O. made it up and stood on the third try. She reeked from the liquor and emanated the same need-a-shower stink as Tower. "I'll tell you what, T.O. We both need to clean up. If you don't mind, I'll take you by your place, let you shower and get some clothes. Then, we'll run by my office and I'll do the same."

T.O. said, "I know what you're doing. You don't want me out of your sight. Right?"

"Well, that, plus you can't drive right now. Your car is okay. We'll pick it up tomorrow. I left you with a college roommate. What happened?"

T.O. glanced away from a wall mirror and rubbed the smudge from her forehead. "I ditched her."

Tower had a long talk with the owner, paid him a bit of money as a deposit on the damages, and joined T.O. at his car. The same sense moved through him like the crime scene where Preston was found. There, and now the bar, Tower thought someone was watching. A crowd had gathered outside the bar and people were small-talking about T.O.'s exploits. Tower went back inside the bar.

"When this all started, was there one person who took more interest than anyone else?"

The owner ran his hands through his hair. "I don't know. I was so busy with her, I didn't notice who was in the place."

"I need a favor. Can you burn me a copy of your surveillance video? Inside and out."

"I can't do it till midnight. I can get you a copy tomorrow."

"Great. I'll be back."

Outside, Tower snap-gazed the street, left to right. He had the same feeling again that someone was watching. More than someone, it was the killer, stalking T.O. and watching her movements. He made a mental check to find out. Hours later, he dropped her off and spent the night going over what facts he had, finally sleeping in his clothes until the cell phone rang.

A groggy Tower answered. "Tower..."

"Morning. Sorry to bother you. It's Ray."

"What's up, Ray."

"I'm up here at the restaurant setting up. Down the way at the pier."

"Yeah...the pier?"

"Well, don't know what's happening, but you better get down there."

12

She was facing east, toward the sun.

Up over the Atlantic and pushing a brilliance on Stilton Bay, morning sun rays lit up the city pier, and a single figure stood alone on the aged, hard wooden planks.

The body of Saneele Gunson.

She was propped up against a concrete post, eyes open, and strangely holding a fishing pole as if waiting for a catch. The sun glare seared every section of the pier, the seldom-used bench and the now dead-pale complexion of Gunson. A soft wind blew across the pier, making her hair flow backward, yet she remained still as a rock, with hands on the pole and frozen in position.

Frank Tower eased his binoculars from his eyes and surveyed the build-up of another crime scene. Mark David was in the middle of a wave of crime techs and his team. Yellow crime tape blocked any entry to the pier. Off to Tower's right, Clay Olson, who ran the bait shop, was arguing with an officer. Olson appeared to be demanding access to his shop where he stored scores of live shrimp and cut squid. The bait was a golden necessity for fishermen looking for the next big catch.

Down to the south, a rain cloud was just offshore of Miami. The cloud resembled a wall of gray mist. Above Tower, loud seagulls swirled flight patterns. Heavy pelicans swooped low, inches above the water, splashing down for a meal. The pelicans were close to shore where the waters were turquoise. Farther away, waves were almost purple. The deeper the water, the darker the color. Tower moved himself close enough to get a good view of Gunson with the help of his binoculars.

Tower could see her eyes looked to be fixed open, like Preston. He couldn't swear to it, but she seemed to have the same punctures to the areas around the eyes and on her nose. Two ropes held her tight to the cement stanchion. Tower feared rigor mortis might make her rigid enough to stand so erect. The condition would give detectives an accurate time of her death. Tower was also processing why she was placed at the pier and in a position like she was fishing. Preston was found at the park. Both victims were staged in a public place. Tower did not have all the facts, yet it appeared she was not kept captive nearly as long as Preston. The killer was moving up his timeline.

A loud scream pierced the brine-scented air.

The same woman who was at Gunson's house was here, dropping down to the ground, falling out of the grasp of a police officer. She squatted down in a heap, letting emotions flow. Two others rushed to help get her standing. Once up, she was escorted away from the pier.

Gunson herself appeared as if she were looking over the march of waves rolling in and settling down in the beige sand. Tower felt a gentle nudge at his side.

"Hi, Frank, this is bad. Really bad."

"Ray, who's watching the restaurant?"

"Got my staff. Only got a few minutes. Have to get back. These people, Frank. They were customers of mine. I've known Saneele for years."

"When was the last time you saw her?"

"She was in last week. I was supposed to cater her luncheon, her monthly Wednesday affair. Twenty-five meals, all with desserts. Then I got the phone call not to come."

A crowd had gathered. All of them standing to see a corpse. He did not see T.O. and knew he had to check on her later. Unfortunately, the body had to stay uncovered until the crime techs were done with their work. Working a crime scene took time. A van arrived and three people were bringing in the tent to block any view from the public. Tower took about sixty photographs, including pics of those standing and watching. He also, best as he could, got photographs of how the rope was tied at the stanchion. Tower knew he might be just a bit too far away. Also, he wanted the brand name of the fishing rod. He knew all these things would be noted and tracked down by Mark David.

Tower moved closer to the stairs of the pier. The place was built forty years earlier and had to be rebuilt in parts because of hurricane damage. There was no lock and the pier was open at all hours. There just weren't any surveillance cameras. He got the attention of Mark David, who nodded in a direction away from the ears of the crowd.

"I know you can't say much," Tower started. "But you might want to talk to Ray, the restaurant owner."

"Thanks." Mark David looked down for a moment to where his shoes started to sink in the soft sand. "I know what you're about to say, Frank. We simply let her down. We didn't get to her before the clock ran out."

"Right now the killer holds all the cards. Mark, you did all you could. Your team should know that. Everything you can learn from this scene will help you pull this jerk off the street." Tower decided to push it. "Can you say if they found another thumb drive?"

"We don't know yet. Have to wait until the autopsy. I can't say much and they'll have my ass if they find out I told you this, but you were right on some things at her house." He walked away.

"Right? About which things?" He just saw the back of Mark David moving to the pier. Tower moved in front of him. Both men stopped. Tower pointed to the body on the pier. "I can see what he's doing. From Preston in the morgue and now here, this guy is sewing up their mouth and nose, then he's watching them suffocate. He's getting off on seeing them die."

Mark David paused and looked as if he wanted to say something. Tower made one more point. "It's obvious he's not killing them here. He's holding them somewhere. You might want to get your guys on warehouses and places away from other homes."

"We're on it, Frank." Mark David stepped away.

"Are you Frank Tower?" A soft voice came from Tower's left. "I'm Saneele's best friend. Janine Iwan."

"I remember you." Tower let out a sigh like he was letting go years of bad times. "I have not seen you in maybe twenty years."

"How's your mother?"

"You mean Jackie? She's okay, I guess."

Tower's bad times were recounted to himself over and over so much, they took the form of nightmares. Jackie's drug habit and her handling of young Frank Tower were legend. The state, on three occasions, worked to remove Frank from the home, only to be rebuffed in court, thanks to a sharp attorney. There were dozens of visits from social workers. One in particular had a contagious grin and the eyes of a sage. She was standing before him now.

"I'm sorry about your friend, Janine."

"We go back years. I knew her husband. We worked together. Saneele had no enemies. I don't know who would do this to her." She reached for a handkerchief and dabbed at the familiar eyes. Tower remembered how just a touch from her on the shoulder and he felt some of his problems had been lifted, and that maybe Jackie would drop her love for crack. Janine put the hanky away and the eyes became defiant. "I want the son of a bitch who killed her."

"She say anything about someone, anyone, who would harm her?"

"No. We were just planning this big luncheon. We were gonna talk orchids, foliage, how to grow roses. Everything Saneele liked."

There was a silence. The empty space lasted several minutes. Tower gave her a chance to decompress. "There was one thing." Her brow bunched up as if she was pooling her thoughts. "She mentioned that maybe someone was outside her place, watching her."

"Did she see who it was?"

"No. Just that when she looked out a window, she saw a man running away. That was it. No real description. Just this guy with a hat or something. She couldn't get a good look at him."

"She report it to anyone?"

The brow lines were no longer taut. "I don't think so. I feel guilty now."

"Don't feel that way. What you can do is say something now. You see that guy over there? That's Detective Mark David. Tell him everything you told me."

"I will." The warm eyes returned. "I heard you were a police officer."

"Was is the operative word."

"And now you investigate on your own." There was a look of pride moving into her face. "I knew what you went through. The times you were left alone. There was a time when I thought about trying to raise you myself."

"Thanks. I appreciate everything you did. One more thing about the man outside. Did Saneele say if she saw a car? Van? Anything?"

"No. Just that he ran and when she looked again, he was gone."

A team from the medical examiner's office moved Saneele's body from the pier. There was quiet. Even the birds stopped moving. They carried her on a board to the unmarked black van. They closed the doors and she was gone.

"Guess I better find that Mr. David." She blinked back a tear.

"Take care." Tower set a path around the parking lot where police had blocked off the entire area and started to trudge through the sand back to his car. His cell phone rang.

"Tower..."

"It's the Sunset Bar. I've got your video cued up if you want it."

13

Tower sat in front of two very dusty video monitors. The video was in black and white. Tower requested and got a cleaning rag to wipe off the screens.

"I know. I don't dust much." The man was bald, heavy-set, with a stomach protruding over his belt.

"No problem. You look at this?"

"No." He moved toward the door. "Listen, I've got deliveries com'n and I gotta git ready for the noon crowd. You okay by yourself?"

"Yeah, I'm fine."

"One other thing. I knew T.O. from when she used to come in here. Haven't seen her in a while. I would never call the cops on her. Just wanted you to know that."

"No problem." Tower was alone with the video equipment. He moved the time stamp to well before T.O. entered the bar and started looking. Tower recognized most of the people in the video. A few he even arrested when he wore blue. When T.O. walked into the place, he wrote the time down in a notebook. She sat at the bar and the two people serving knew her. They exchanged small-talk, then T.O. started drinking. Tower saw the hesitation in her face when she took the first sip. Several minutes passed with T.O. insisting on another drink. Then another. There was some argument and she was given the bottle. A large group pushed through the door.

Tower almost glossed over their entrance as it looked as normal as all the others, then he noticed something. He paused, then backed up the video several times. He watched their entry again and again. Finally, Tower spotted something odd.

When the group entered the bar, a person showed up on the screen, out on the street. He or she, it was hard to make out. Tower took out his cell phone and took a shot of the person on the monitor. He tried to blow up the picture only to find the image became a blurry mess. Tower couldn't tell age, sex, height. Nothing. For the next forty minutes, he studied the smudge on the screen. He only knew one thing: the person was watching. Inside the bar, a waiter made his routine visits to the table, making sure the group was satisfied with drinks and some food. When the group was finished and walked out the door, Tower took notice of the time.

The blurry image of a person was gone.

Tower scanned another twenty minutes and found video of himself entering the bar. Again, he took down the time stamps.

The bar owner came back into the room. "You find anything?"

"A bit. So, this my copy of the video?"

"Yep. All yours."

"Thanks. Do me a favor and please call Detective Mark David and give him the same video. Is that okay?"

"No problem."

Tower left the bar with the video. He had another stop to make.

Tower drove around T.O.'s apartment twice, then stopped and did surveillance for thirty minutes before he knocked on her door.

She looked much better than the booze-induced version in the storage room. "Thanks for coming to my rescue." T.O. snapped off the top of a bottle of water.

"I think someone is following you. Any strange faces anywhere?"

"No. Just the regulars." She chugged more water.

"Just be careful. I can't put a fix on it but just look around when you go in and out."

"You getting anywhere on Preston?"

"Nothing I can say. I'm working on a couple of things. The reason I'm here is to check on you." Tower watched her down the rest of the bottle. "You supposed to be at work?"

"They gave me a few days of advanced vacation."

Tower checked out her window for the seventh time when his cell chimed in.

"Tower..."

"I need you down here ASAP." Mark David sounded worried. "Here. Now. Okay?"

14

Tower always considered the Stilton Bay police station as being an afterthought. One mile north of the glitzy downtown shopping area, the place was almost out of the city. Once a city garage, the police department was converted, or as Tower once said, regurgitated into a lockup, office floors of homicide, robbery, and general meeting rooms. A large side building was added to house a shooting range. The four-story PD, with its aged-looked pinkish stucco, was next to the just-about-new morgue and medical examiner's office.

Strange, thought Tower, parking in the visitors' lot. For five years, he worked here, knew all the cracks in the floor to avoid. When a monsoon-style Florida rain gushed through the drains, he knew where to walk around the temporary waterfalls. Now he had to enter through the front door.

Tower walked through the metal detector set up in the lobby and waited. The wait was not long.

"We're in here." Mark David swiped his card, allowing both of them to enter the matrix of hallways leading to several meeting areas. David turned left, away from the homicide office.

He entered a room with most of the lights turned off.

Mark David's unit was there. They looked just as pensive as the last time Tower saw them.

"Show him." Mark David pointed to a computer screen. Jake May let his finger hover over a button.

"What is this?" Tower looked to David for some clue.

Mark David again pointed to the screen. "We don't have much time. We got another message. The only reason you're here, again I'm sad to say, is because this killer has singled you out."

Tower pushed. "Where did you find it? During the autopsy?"

"What's important now is we show you this and we get moving." David sounded impatient.

The button was pushed.

On the screen Tower saw the message:

YOU ARE NOT TELLING FRANK TOWER EVERYTHING. SHARE EVERYTHING WITH HIM. YOU HAVE LESS TIME TO FIGURE IT OUT

A clock appeared. The wind-down was already in motion, showing what appeared to be less than twelve hours. And counting.

Mark David stood in front of Tower. "We've got less than twelve hours to find this guy. Gunson, as you pointed out, was asphyxiated. Her lips and nose were sewn shut. Obviously, this information will not be shared with the press since this is known, we think, only to the killer. You said this guy is taking great steps to watch them die. Somehow, he is convinced we're not giving you a lot of information. And he's right, we're not. How he knows that, I am not sure. Somehow, we have to make him think you know everything."

Tower pitched an idea. "Why don't you let me go with you somewhere. Anywhere. Maybe he's watching. If he sees me out there with you, there's a chance he'll screw up."

"We can do that. It doesn't mean we'll actually share any information with you, but we can give it the appearance that you're part of this. Maybe that will draw him out."

"I like it. You want to start now?"

"The clock is not stopping, so we won't either." Mark David turned on all the lights in the room. "Especially since we have one thing we're about to make public."

Tower got up to leave. "And?"

"We have a person of interest. A suspect. We're releasing the name in one hour."

15

While the others filed out of the room, Tower pulled Mark David aside. "A suspect? Who?"

"One of the names you gave me. It checks out he was in the vicinity of the two victims. He has a history with you and right now he's missing."

"The name?"

"Stan Brady."

Tower remembered him. "He ran a scam, pretending he was hurt on the job. When I surveilled him, it took me two weeks before he slipped up and was walking around without a cast on his arm. Fake injury and fake prescriptions. He got drugs and sold them on the street. The state attorney didn't think we, I should say the department, had enough evidence. They let it go. But he was fired from his job."

Mark David left the room. "C'mon. I have two teams. One outside Brady's house. The other with me, checking out where he usually goes. The public doesn't know this is time-sensitive, but we're releasing a photograph of Brady and calling him a person we want to speak with."

Tower rode with Mark David. They parked outside a car repair shop two blocks from T-Town. Tower fidgeted. "You sure this is the best use of our time?"

Mark David gripped the wheel. "As opposed to what?"

"I think Brady is about six-five. Big guy. He's able to run a scam, but killer? I don't think so."

"I know physical harm is not in his background, but the group thinks this is the best direction."

Tower persisted. "I don't think he's your guy."

"Then who is?"

Tower considered giving up what little facts he had. The thumb drive clock winding down was enough to convince Tower to speak. "I've been trailing a guy who is watching two people. Close friends of your two victims. I think this guy is getting his rocks off watching them in grief. He, I believe, has been trailing them so he can watch and enjoy seeing them in pain."

"You've seen this guy?"

"Well, not really. I saw some video, surveillance from the Sunset Bar, and I was working up a case on whether this person was stalking my client. The video doesn't show much. Can't make out anything. What I know about Brady is he does drugs. I don't think he would take the time to torture victims and sew up their mouths. That's just not Brady."

"Tell ya what. Why don't we take Brady in, speak to him, and my guys will tell if he's the one or not. We're running out of time." Mark David stared at Tower. "Sure you never saw this character, the one you say was outside the bar?"

"No. It was all blurry."

They waited twenty minutes.

Mark David's phone rang. "Yeah." He listened for a good thirty seconds, then put the phone away. "We're needed somewhere else."

"Where?"

"You'll know."

Stan Brady's house was a short sixteen minutes away. Two other unmarked cars were already there. In all, three detectives sat watching a home. The place looked like a swollen lip. A red-bottomed boat was leaning up against the house on its side. Long scrapes along its hull told of a history of misuse.

A rusted Mercury outboard was summarily left in a large tub. The last grass cutting was probably a year earlier. Big shafts of dollar weed and crabgrass claimed most of the front yard.

Mark David got out of his car. He turned to Tower. "Just a few minutes here and you're free. If he's gonna see you, it will be here."

Tower moved to a spot in the shade under a tree.

Mark David and Detective May approached the door. The street was calm.

David knocked. A long minute went by. Tower could hear everything and his only thought was the clock.

A tall, thin black woman answered. She had torn shorts and a short-sleeve blouse covering her tapered body.

"We didn't call the police." Her words had the low, husky timbre of a smoker's voice.

Mark David looked past her, into the house, as he spoke. "Is Stan Brady here?"

"Stan ain't done anything to git the po-po's attention." She moved the door closed two inches.

"We'd just like to speak with him, that's all. Is he here?"

"Nope. Not right now. He's out closing a deal on Wall Street." The soft rumble of her laugh cascaded out across the yard in Tower's direction.

Mark David eased any possible tension in his voice. "Is it okay with you if we take a look inside? Just a quick look and I'm gone."

"The last time a man said that to me all nice, I almost got pregnant." She opened the door. "Since you seem kind, I'll let you in. Just you."

Mark David opened the door as far as it could go. He walked inside the place. She went with him.

From outside, Tower saw images of two people through the dingy curtains. They moved from the front to the rear bedrooms and back until he heard David bumping into something metallic in the backyard. Another three minutes later, he emerged through the front door.

She licked her lips. "Well, aren't you gonna give me your card? I might need to call you."

Mark David gave her a card and walked on the cracked walkway to the

curb. He said a few words to May and left him there, then motioned to
Tower to get in the car. "You're done being a decoy. Taking you back."

"No problem."

Tower considered one more push to convince Mark David he was
wrong about Brady. Every investigative intuition in his body said David was
wasting time. Every second spent on a bad lead could mean the next victim
was closer to being in jeopardy.

Tower got into his own car and drove toward his office. He raked
through the list of possible avenues he could follow to find the man in the
bar. He was just two blocks from his office door when he noticed a white
male walking away from him. The man turned around, and took off
running. Tower turned around too and followed, kicking up his speed. The
figure turned down a path between two houses. Tower got out on foot and
gave chase.

He was running after Stan Brady.

16

Ten steps into the run, Tower learned Brady was a lot faster than him. A half-block and Tower was losing ground. Maybe he should have stayed in his car. Ahead of him, Brady turned a corner and ran into a woman carrying a cloth bag of groceries. She was able to hold on to the bag, and Brady, for a moment, was slowed down. Tower closed in. Just as he was within ten yards, Brady ran through the parking lot of Ray's Restaurant. This time, a collision caused the maintenance man to lose his balance and fall hard to the pavement. Tower had no choice. He stopped to give aid.

"You okay?"

The man rolled over and sat up, examining two small cuts on his arm. "Yeah, I'm fine."

Brady was gone.

Ray came out of the back door holding a wet rag, handing it to his employee.

"Sorry, Ray. I was chasing somebody."

Ray helped the guy to his feet and he went back inside the restaurant. "Frank, nothing you do surprises me. What did this guy do?"

"Police want to talk to him."

Ray slapped his pants hard. "The guy on the news?"

"Yeah, that's him. I should leave the chasing to the police."

Twenty seconds later, two unmarks rolled up. Mark David got out, quickly scanning the area. In the second car, Jake May emerged, along with Sania Powell. James Corker got out of his own unit. Three police cars pulled up, officers getting out, doors slamming, all walking with a sense of urgency, adrenalin in their faces. Tower knew the feeling well.

"You almost got him?" Corker's decibel-busting voice carried over the hum of a gathering crowd.

Tower rubbed his right knee. "Guess I'm not as fast as I used to be."

Corker moved in close on Tower. "You let him get away."

Mark David stared down Corker. "He doesn't wear a badge anymore. He's not obligated to catch anyone."

"He's a P.I." Corker spat out the words. "Pathetic individual."

David let the words die in the air a full thirty seconds, then waved Corker back to his car. He turned to Tower. "We're under a lot of pressure. The chief, the mayor, everyone wants some results, and what the public doesn't know, but we do, is that our time is running out. Stan Brady could have been a good lead for us. We've got the area sectioned off. We'll catch him."

"What if you're chasing down the wrong lead?"

"So, we're back to that again? Can you answer me this, why would he run from you?"

"I don't know, Mark. He knows bad things happen when people want to question him."

The crowd started to break up. Two of the patrol cars moved off. Corker and the other detectives left. Only Mark David and Tower remained. David looked at the back door area. "No cameras here."

"The guy he knocked down didn't see anything. I'm pretty sure of it. Had his back turned. You're right, I'm not police anymore. I have to be careful chasing somebody down as a civilian, especially if my life hasn't been threatened."

Mark David checked his watch twice. "Don't worry. I'd vouch for you. C'mon. I'll give you a ride back to your car. You can give that bum knee a rest."

"You're worried about the timeline."

"Frank, every person on the force is working on this. All vacations have been canceled. We have to find an answer in all this."

17

T.O. kept clenching her fists, anger building up in her hotter than spilled lava. "That's the guy?" The wide-screen television was showing a picture of Stan Brady.

"They just want to talk to him." Tower carefully considered his next few words. "He's not charged with anything. They just want to rule him out."

"Then why is he on the run? Just talk to police." T.O. looked around as if she was looking for something to throw.

"This guy had some throw-downs with police. I don't know his sheet. Maybe he's afraid of VOP. A violation of probation means instant jail."

"I just want to talk to him myself." T.O.'s fist looked like a knuckled mallet. Her heavy breathing reminded him of a boxer.

"T.O., the best thing for you is to let police grab him up. You're just going to drive up your blood pressure."

She picked up a blue pillow and threw the thing at the wall next to her. "Okay! I didn't break anything." She picked it up again. "I just want to meet this asswipe." She pushed the pillow up to her mouth and sat down in the folding cushions of the couch.

"I'm here to give you an update."

For the first time, she took her gaze away from the television. "Update?"

"I'm being told they are releasing Preston's body in two days. That means if you wanted to plan any burial service, now is the time to start." As he talked, Tower checked his watch. He knew the countdown clock was moving and there was no apparent progress in finding the next victim before there was another kidnapping. "You also should be watching carefully for anything strange. I think someone was watching you at the bar. Watching you grieve over Preston."

"That is one sick person. And you're sure it wasn't Brady?"

"You can't identify the guy in the video. Too blurry. I'm just going on a few facts. Brady is a schemer, yes, but blood and torture I don't think are part of his game plan. He's a con man, not a killer. But that's just my opinion."

T.O. sat there for a few minutes absorbing what she was hearing. The pillow was tucked into the couch. The closed fist opened up. She leaned back and turned off the television. "So, what do you plan to do?"

"This guy uses public places to position his victims. Right now, I don't see his pattern, just that they are all public. I've got to do some surveillance. Just pick a spot and wait."

"You need my help?"

"You just stay right here. Away from any troubles and no bars." Tower got up to leave. He looked out the window. Even though there was some distance, Tower could make out the skyline of the business district. Dusk was close and the hot glare was no more. The late afternoon sun was in a downward slide and the buildings were basked in an amber radiance.

Tower's phone rang. "Tower..."

"Listen, I already called the police. They checked and didn't find anything. Hope you don't mind. I Googled your business number."

"Janine?"

"Yes. If you don't mind, could you come over? I think someone's been in my backyard."

∾

Sixteen minutes later Tower was in front of a one-story standard stucco home, Florida style. The grass had just been trimmed and the pathway to the door was lined with salvia. Just a hint of the sun remained and darkness was claiming the sky.

Janine Iwan opened the door before Tower got there. "Please come in." As she walked, her fingers pushed strands of gray-black hair into place. Fear was not in her face, just concern. She pointed to a photo album. "I was looking through some old pictures of Saneele and me, going back almost fifteen years, and I heard some noises coming from the backyard. I turned out the lights and looked. There was definitely someone there."

Tower pulled out his cell phone and found a photograph of Stan Brady. "Was it him?"

"No. Well, maybe. But I really couldn't see his face. But there was a bunch of movement through my croton bushes. Then it got quiet. I called police and they came. Inspected everything and left."

"I can check out there, if you want?"

"Thanks. That would be great. I feel like I should be paying you or something."

Tower followed her through the house to the back door. "Don't worry about it. All the things you did for me as a kid, I really owe you."

"At Social Services, you don't know the big debates we had on whether to pull you out of that environment. But your mother kept promising she would change. Stop the drugs. So we kept you there."

"She didn't stop. At least not right away. I remember you bought shoes for me one time."

"Shoes, some shirts, anything you needed, I got you. I was supposed to report your mom's shortcomings but I left that out."

Tower stepped down three steps to a circular pattern of bricks about eighteen feet in diameter. Two patio chairs and a small table were set off to the right.

He moved slow and studied the yard.

Tower pulled out a flashlight and continued his search. The brick was edged in plants. Croton and red Ti plants. Another twenty yards away was the fence. Tower stood out on the grass and looked into Janine's house. There was a clear direct view of her at the couch where she would be studying the photo album. There were a few impressions in the dirt, but

Tower knew they could have come from the police officers making their check.

He went to the gate. Tower's light focused on a piece of cloth stuck in the gate lever. Tower moved in closer and pulled out his cell phone. Seven to ten snaps later he was done with the photographs. He left the cloth there without touching it. Maybe it meant something. Maybe not. The cloth could be from a shirt or a jacket. He went back inside.

"I don't want to alarm you but I want you to be careful. More careful than usual." Tower made sure the door was locked. "If you don't have a security system, I recommend you get one. Even a camera. When you leave the house, look around before you get in the car, even leave the phone in a ready position to call 9-1-1. When you leave, circle the block a couple of times. See if there is any movement at your house. If you do, don't, and I repeat don't, approach anyone. Go to a safe spot and call police. When you get home, do the same thing. Circle the block a few times to make sure no one is following you. Then park. And please, you can call me at any time. Day or night."

"Thanks, Frank."

"There's a good chance someone was out there."

The photo album was tucked under her arm. "If you knew Saneele, you would do anything for her. We had so much fun talking about plants. She didn't know it but we were going to surprise her with a sort of award. But..."

"From what I'm seeing, everyone liked her."

Janine's expression told him she went to a place known only to herself. "When we were young, about eight or so, we decided we would climb a tree. I wasn't very good at it, so she went first. She went from a lower to the higher branch with ease. Then came my turn. I got about five feet up and I started to lose my grip. I knew I was going to drop. She was just a bit higher than me, but she dropped out of the tree on purpose, landing hard on the ground. When I lost my grip, I fell into her arms. She braced my fall. She was all scratched up and hurt for a week, but I was okay. The only thing she wanted to do was to protect me. That's Saneele. I think about her death every minute and it hurts."

"Just hold on to those memories. I'll see myself out."

Tower called Mark David the minute he was behind the wheel and strapped in. "I know you are busy, Mark, but I just left Janine's house."

"I saw the call. She okay?"

"Yes, but someone left a piece of clothing on the gate going into the backyard. I didn't touch it, but your folks might want to look at it."

"Thanks. I'll get an officer to patrol her area more often."

"She would appreciate it."

18

Mark David reached for his cup of coffee and almost spat it out since the brew was cold. When he got up to refresh the cup, he walked into a buzz of activity. Two detectives on the phone in loud conversations, trying to make links to the victims. Sania Powell led a team dedicated to taking phone calls from the public and following up on leads. James Corker was in the field leading another group doing stakeouts and examining surveillance camera video. Big Jake May was assigned to creating a profile of the last hours of movement by Stan Brady and all the victims. They had an hour before all of them would converge on a meeting to discuss what they found. The killer's countdown clock was removed from the room. Mark David knew every second passing meant another person was getting closer to becoming a victim. The lost time without a suspect was starting to wear on him like a vise squeezing the life out of their investigation.

"Damn clock!" Sania met him at the coffee maker. "I try not to think about it."

"Then don't." David stirred the all-black brew. "You have the clock. I have the chief and the vice-mayor calling for updates."

"Nice. This whole thing is my new life. I eat, sleep this investigation. Let me correct that. I don't sleep."

Mark David took another swig. "The thing about the clock. It's not the deadline for a death. It's the deadline for taking someone. So, even when the clock is zero, we still have a chance of finding them."

They left the coffee area and headed back to their respective desks. David allowed himself a quick glance at his watch. Less than two hours and counting down. He went over the autopsy reports for the twentieth time, hoping to pull one detail and see it in another vein. The phone call records came back for Stan Brady that showed he called and texted his girlfriend, but none of the victims. However, Brady was caught on two surveillance cameras in the general area of both kidnap scenes. Either he was the killer or maybe he was just watching. The sad thing was Brady managed to get through their net and was loose to do whatever. The computer taken from Preston's apartment showed no valuable evidence.

Mark David couldn't tell Frank Tower that he found circle rings on a kitchen counter in Saneele Gunson's home. Gunson was not a drinker and sipped from a certain mug much larger than the circles.

The urgency was oppressive. Every second that ticked off was a second lost.

Sania Powell pulled up a chair next to Mark David's desk. Jake May sat on the other side of him. James Corker called in and would be on speaker. "Anyone want to go first?" David wiped dust from a yellow pad and prepared to write.

"I'll go." Sania looked at her notes. "We got a few calls claiming they spotted Brady. The problem is those claims put him in three different places at the same time. We're tracking it down. A lot of people either know him or worked with him briefly. I say briefly 'cause after the workman's comp deal, most places won't hire him. We're still working it."

"Thanks." David finished writing some notes. "Corker?"

"We're set up on three places: his home, around Ray's Restaurant, and the park in downtown. We're still playing that hunch that he likes to stash his victims in a very public location, like the pier. Still nothing, but we're ready."

"Thanks, James. Jake?"

"Well, we know a lot about Gunson's movements, but not Preston. He was supposed to meet up with his friend T.O. but never showed. We now think he was taken from his apartment. And there's water circles, but nothing else on them. We also noted a missing photograph."

Mark David stopped him. "Was anything taken from Gunson's place?"

"She has so much stuff, it's hard to tell."

David swallowed the last of the coffee. "What if we get her friend over there for a supervised visit to the place. What's her name, Janine, might see something we missed. Jake, can you set that up?"

"Will do." He checked his list. "We're working under the theory that both victims were being stalked prior to the taking, so we're also going through as much area surveillance as we can to try and come up with a face. Something for facial rec."

Mark David did something he regretted. He looked at his watch. The group got quiet. "Sorry about that. I know, I know, we don't have a lot of time. This clock thing is worse than the heat. Go back to work. If anyone has something to report, let me know and I'll make the group aware. Any questions?"

They got up. David closed down the phone call to James Corker. The clock was working against them.

19

Frank Tower parked his surveillance van in a dark spot across the street from Janine Iwan's house. He had set up the van with portals for shooting video, a desk with a computer, black-out curtains, and a small privy. Tower could stay here for several hours. From his location, he was able to watch for anyone trying to get access to the back gate or watch through a front window. Two front windows were rolled down one-third so he could hear any movement. His Glock rested on the desk.

One hour into his stay he thought about moving to T.O.'s apartment. His plan was to move back and forth between both places, looking for anyone sneaking or peeking. T.O. was a client and deserved his attention right now. Janine was one of the people who probably saved him from being a victim in the streets. He owed her his time.

Tower's phone thumped. "Hello, Shannon."

"Thought I'd catch you before you went to bed." Her voice was silky just like the first day he met her. She was running after her wind-blown hat on the beach. Tower tracked it down and started a conversation. A conversation that ended in a wedding months later. Now, he was repairing the damage after an affair a year earlier.

"I'm out on a case."

"This late? I thought with me out of the house you'd invite some dancing girls. I hear they bring their own pole these days."

"No girls. No poles. Just watching a house. I'm in the van."

"All night?"

"Looks that way. It's important."

"I heard something about it up here. I won't keep you long.

I just wanted to let you know I will be back in two days. My car is at the airport. I'll be fine."

"I'm gonna make you a promise."

She sounded excited. "A promise? I like it."

"A vacation. On an island. Plenty of room to search the beach and dinner at sunset."

"I like. When?"

"When this case is over. We'll sit down. Plan it out. I have an island in mind."

"Can't wait."

Tower watched a raccoon scamper across the street. "Let me know when you get back. Dinner at Ray's."

"Sounds great. Have fun sleeping in the van. Bye."

Tower put the phone down and again concentrated on the house. Two more hours into his watch, only the animals were in the street. Close to dawn, he let himself sleep for a couple of hours. He knew the deadline given to police was past.

20

On the third drop-off of wood, Roland Kincade thrust a right hand to his side. "Dammit." The pain shot up into his armpit. For two minutes, he shook his hand as if that might ease the throbbing. Kincade looked at the finished pile of stacked wood. Almost done. He still needed to move a rough stack he had just purchased the day before. The Friday morning sun was up and working on a midday heat for anyone delirious enough to work in the sticky humidity.

"You win." Kincade walked away from the pile and sat on the truck bed of his SUV. The trunk lid was up and protected him from the sun's blaze. Kincade's life was a simple affair. Divorced and retired, he seldom traveled, dated a bit, exercised as little as possible, and spent hours cooking a good meal. He was still rubbing his side when a hand came up around his face and pushed a rag hard against his nose and mouth.

He tried to talk and grabbed the hand to push the rag away. Kincade's world was starting to fade. The chemical smell he was experiencing made him sleepy. He started kicking, swinging his arms, anything to get free of the rag. His right shoe flew off in the subdued melee. His house, the wood pile, his vision was starting to shut down and go black. Kincade's left arm dropped like a ham on a kitchen counter.

He was out.

The figure pulled him into the SUV and left him there on the trunk bed. Gloved hands reached Kincade's pockets and found the keys to the car. The trunk lid was closed, and when the SUV drove off, the drive was as casual as a trip to the store. Three minutes later, the SUV stopped near an open field. The place was free of any walkers or potential witnesses. The figure, balaclava over his head and face, pulled Kincade out, hefted him up, and pushed him into a panel van. Kincade lay there, arms sprawled out like he was a beached whale.

One, then a second can of fuel were placed on the grass instead of the ground. The figure moved the panel van up a few yards, got out with a broom, and started to sweep any tire tracks or shoe prints left behind. Splashes of fuel were doused all over Roland Kincade's SUV. The car was covered inside and out with liquid. The cans were tossed inside the SUV. The gloved figure looked around. No one was in the vicinity. He removed matches from his pocket and lit four of them before tossing the entire box into the nearby SUV. Flames started to eat away at the black leather and dashboard. The warmth of the heat reached out.

When he got back to the panel van, the figure again swept away any tracks, got inside, and drove off. From his rearview mirror, he watched the abandoned SUV. Arms of flames reached into the back seat, dashboard, and driver's area. The figure was mesmerized by the ever-growing fire. He liked to watch. There were tasks to be done, meaning he could not stay till the end. Time to move on. Ninety seconds later, he watched in the mirror as the SUV exploded into a fireball.

The figure looked back at Kincade and smiled.

21

Roland Kincade woke to the smell of someone's urine. He looked and realized the bucket near him needed to be emptied. When he tried to get up from the chair, he could not. His hands were handcuffed to a pole behind him. The chair he was sitting in was bolted to the floor. A neck restraint limited how much he could move and he soon learned his new range of motion was very small. There were no windows and the walls were covered in handprints.

"Hey! Let me out!" No reply. Kincade blinked a few times as he went through the last moments before he went blank. He could picture stacking the wood and sitting on the truck, yet the rest was not there.

On the far wall, well out of his reach, two very large speakers were on either side of the door. The door itself looked more than solid enough to keep him captive. The speakers were the only other items in the small space besides the bucket. There was no way to figure out where he was or the time. His watch was gone. A familiar pain returned. His side hurt and he was not able to rub the painful area.

Kincade looked around the room again. This time, he noticed a very small camera in the corner, near the ceiling.

He was being watched.

The speakers came alive. Extremely loud music blasted at him. There was no rhythmic cadence, just a blare of nonsensical guitar playing and erratic drums.

Kincade shut his eyes. If he could, he would have covered his ears with his hands. He sat in the chair like a sailor trying to withstand huge waves on the ocean during a storm. For Kincade, the waves were a jumbled mix of bad notes coming at him in high volume.

Then, the blare stopped.

With no way to check, he knew his heartbeat must be up. He couldn't feel his cell phone that was always tucked away in his right pocket. He felt alone and vulnerable. Without any warning, the high-octane noise started again. There was no way he would be able to sleep. The crash of sounds lasted another fifteen minutes as far as he could tell. He was now worn out and tired. And thirsty.

He appealed to the camera. "I need water. I can pay you. Whatever you want, just give me a number. Just let me go." The camera was unyielding.

Kincade moved against his restraints. He pulled hard on the neck tie and started to choke. He gave up and instead yanked on the handcuffs. He pulled until he felt his skin starting to chafe. He was hungry, thirsty, and again worn down. Kincade let his breathing even out. He half expected the noise to restart. He had no guestimate on time, yet it seemed hours went by.

The door opened.

A man dressed in all black entered with his face covered and some device on his chest. "Do you know why you are here?" The voice was all garbled and sounded mechanical.

"Just let me go. I can't see your face. I won't tell anyone."

The robotic voice was not moved. "You're here for one purpose. And you will serve that purpose." The man walked toward him. "If you don't comply, you will be beaten. You understand?"

"I don't understand why I'm here. I don't know you. Where are we?"

"You are serving a purpose." The man untied the neck restraint, eased Kincade to his feet, and guided him to a gurney. "Lay down."

"I'm fine. I don't need to lay down."

The punch to Kincade's stomach made him flinch and hold it for several seconds. The pain rippled through him like lightning and made his side hurt again. He moved to the gurney.

Once he was prone, Kincade was belted in, strapped down, and unable to move much. The figure moved him down the hallway. Kincade's eyes darted all over the place, trying to figure out where he was and if he recognized the hallway. He also listened for anyone in the place. The building was stone quiet. As the gurney was pushed into another room, he did see that he was moving past several rooms. Kincade ruled out a school. The gurney stopped in a large room with high ceilings.

Kincade panicked.

On a nearby table were cutting tools, blades and knives of all sizes, three drills, and a few bottles of unknown liquids. Kincade started to yell. A cloth was stuffed into his mouth. When Kincade tried to spit out the cloth, the figure stuffed it back in, only deeper. "Stop. I want you awake for this."

Kincade started to shake violently. His legs stretched the straps, his chest rose up against the bracings. The figure just stood back and let Kincade wear himself out.

When he was able to lift up his head, Kincade noticed something. Some fifty feet from him, at the rear of the room, were two large doors. The place now seemed familiar. Kincade was convinced he had been there before. He tried to get a second look by raising up. The move was met with a crack to the head and a warning to stop.

The man with the knives looked at Kincade as if examining a ripe pepper. "Your protesting won't help you. This is your time. Your time to serve your purpose." The figure turned to his vast array of implements. He rolled a tray to the far counter and picked out a few items, placing them carefully on the tray and rolling it back to Kincade's left side. Lights were turned on and Kincade felt the intense heat of the lamps.

The figure leaned in. He held a small, semi-circular needle. Kincade recognized it. A surgical needle. "This might hurt. I'm not giving you anything to ease the pain. I want you to feel this."

Kincade's head snapped from left to right to avoid being touched. The figure grabbed his jaw and held Kincade's head in place, all the while guiding the needle and string toward Kincade's lips.

The mechanical voice sounded like he was laughing. "When this is done, you will be known forever."

22

Frank Tower blinked twice and he was awake, still parked across the street from Iwan's home. He let himself take a nap thinking if Janine Iwan was asleep, there would be no reason for the stalker to be here. Even with that knowledge, Tower did not want to leave until morning. For Tower, the morning sun brought a stiff neck and a sore right knee. He was in desperate need of coffee and a slap of cold water on the face.

Before he got a chance to move, he got a call. "Tower, go ahead."

"Frankie, it's your..." There was a pause. "Jackie. I need your help. Can you stop by here?"

"I'm in the middle of something right now. I really don't have the time to go by there. There's a murder investigation, and a client needs me."

"I need you too. Just a minute. Okay?" Tower said he was on his way and placed the phone in a tray. He wanted to move anyway before Janine noticed his ugly van parked outside.

As he drove into T-Town, the area was quiet. The hustlers were sleeping, just like vampires. Their domain was nighttime, when the money could be made and temptation was sweetened by many swigs on a 40-ounce.

Tower pulled into the parking lot and Jackie almost ran to his van. "We can talk out here."

"We always do. You don't like me inside." Tower closed the door and both of them stood in the shade of the van. "What's wrong?"

She started pulling and twirling a section of her gray-black hair. "I just want you to scare him a little. Just a little. Nothing major."

"Scare who?"

"He's got some of my people so scared, they won't come anymore. They need to continue their sessions. A couple of them are in drug court and if they don't get their certificate, there will be a problem."

"Jackie, you're bouncing all over the place. So, someone is scaring some of your people?"

"Nathan Kasmillin. They call him Nat. He runs the drugs over here and a few of the girls. He's mad 'cause so many people are going into rehab. Out here we just call it 'hab." Jackie wiped a line of sweat from her forehead. "He's losing money." There was a degree of pride in her voice. "He's losing money 'cause they chose 'hab over him. And now, he's on this terror thing to force them to stay away. They're scared."

"Why don't you call police?"

"Police? With all that's going on, my priority level with them is lower than the ground I'm standing on. They ain't got time for me."

"I really don't have time either. I'm on the outside of this investigation and I need to stay focused on that."

She wrapped her arms around herself. "It's because of me, isn't it?"

"It's not really about you. I just don't have time right now. I can't get into all the details but it's life and death."

Her brow lines crinkled up and she pointed a finger at the front doors of the Never Too Late. "You don't think it's life and death for the people in there? They face that every day. It's poison or no poison. Drugs or clean. I got seven people too scared to make it in after a great start. They're all stuck in a room in a drug house on Tella Avenue, trying to figure out how to keep going through withdrawal and recovery. Nat is just sit'n outside, waiting to sell them more shit." She punched at the air. "I'd go over there and punch him out myself, but I can't leave the others here."

"If I can't help you, it's not because of our past."

"It is about our past. I was a bad mother."

"We don't have to go down this road. I really have to go."

She grabbed his arm. "Frankie, if I could, I'd tear the wings off the clock and start over."

"Hands. A clock has hands."

"Hands, arms, legs, Frankie, whatever you call'm, I wish I could just start again. Then, maybe you'd call me mother."

"You had a lot of chances to kick the drugs but we both know you didn't. I'm the same kid who didn't have birthday presents a couple of years because you spent it all on drugs. You turned in your mother card a long time ago."

There was silence between them. Jackie just let her arms go limp, like a fighter ready to throw in the towel. She pushed both hands through the tangle of hair. "Okay, that's fair. You probably had the worst upbringing but I'm still your mother. And I need a favor. I got seven people. Three of them used to be hookers, two guys who kept upping their drug intake until they robbed jus 'bout every house within a square mile and got caught. And a one-time businessman of the year. Man loved his pills. Damn near got himself killed. Called me his last chance. I told him that's why we named the place the Never Too Late." A smile moved across cracked, dry lips.

"Not sure I can do much."

She fired back, "I've got fifty-seven souls coming here. Each year I move almost two hundred people to being drug free." As she spoke, the veins in her neck bulged, her hands jabbed at an imaginary chest to make a point. "These folks are counting on this place, 'cause we don't charge anything to git in. If this Nat piece-a-shit gets his way, more will follow right back to the hole without a bottom. For them, all they got is me and this place. I was a bad somebody back then. I'm sorry about that, Frankie. But I'm trying to make up for it now."

Tower opened the van door. "Where is this place again? I'll make a stop and see what I can do. Can't promise anything. Is that clear?"

She ran to him, again with the goal of a hug, then she stopped and held back. "My Frankie! I love you. You know that."

"Yeah, I know. I'm doing it because they're trying to change. I can respect that."

23

Frank Tower parked the surveillance van in the garage, and spent the next two hours studying the make-up of the homes in that section of Tella Avenue. An online search gave him details about the house. The place was owned by what looked like a shell company. City and county code violations totaled more than fifty over the span of eleven years. Tower noted grass too tall, garbage piling up, broken windows, complaints of strange smells coming from the building. He wanted to know all he could about the home and other residences nearby.

There were also video files showing aerial views of the entire lot. Tower noticed there was a common walkway behind the homes. The house in question on Tella Avenue was on a cul-de-sac, meaning very little car traffic. People cornered in that home would almost be trapped.

Tower checked his watch three times. He listened to the radio for any news of a missing person. He had to fight to keep his thoughts focused on the house, instead of the murder investigation. Then he wondered if the clock deadline had passed and maybe there was no victim. No word from Mark David.

He kept working. Tower got in his car and drove near Tella Avenue. He got out a block from the entrance of the cul-de-sac and pulled up his binoculars. Once he adjusted the binocs, he saw one car parked directly in front of the house. One man was standing outside, leaning up against the car. Two others were inside the all-black SUV. Tower tried but he could not see any movement inside the target house. Then, one man inside the SUV got out carrying a bag of what looked like groceries, headed for the front door. The man didn't knock, he just went inside, came back out empty-handed, and returned to the SUV.

Tower started to form a plan. He pulled up his long-range camera and snapped ten to fifteen shots, including the man walking back to the car, the house, the street, everything. The cul-de-sac was where Tella Avenue ended. The end of the road. Tower got back inside his car. There were two things he needed for his plan. One, he needed help.

Second, he would leave his Glock in the car.

24

A man ambled along Tella Avenue adjusting his backpack. He was wearing two sweaters, way too many clothes for the broil of a Florida summer. He was holy in the sense there were holes in both sweaters, rips in the pants, and a hole in the wool cap on his head. His right sneaker's shoelaces were loose, and anyone getting too close would enter the smell-cloud of body odor tainted with the tang of whiskey.

There was no movement on the street. The air was quiet and empty of any bird noise. The man made a zig-zag path for the SUV, stumbling and stopping, then staring at the sky. There was no cadence to his walk, just the unpredictable stride of someone who had no grip on the world at large.

Inches from the SUV, the man with two sweaters reached out and tried to open the rear passenger door. A large person ballooned out of the car like a ladder unfolding to a great height. He confronted two sweaters.

"Get back, old man. Damn, you stink." The man who got out of the car was around six-five, a good two-hundred-eighty pounds.

A perfectly dirty finger pointed to the big man. "Aren't you my Uber?" Two sweaters laughed with a noticeable slurring of words. The tip of his fingernail was arched in filth.

Big man was getting impatient. "Get back or I'll pound your ass."

Now, two more doors to the SUV opened. Big man was joined by a much smaller man who was also in a back seat. "My name is Nat and I own this block. Get your funky ass back on out. Is that clear?" The third man from the SUV was around six feet tall and kept at a distance away from the others.

"I just want my ride to downtown. That's all." The man with two sweaters took three steps back and sat down. "I think I might pee."

Big man's eyes widened. "Oh no you ain't." He turned to the others. "He'll stink up the whole block."

All the commotion left the three men staring down at two sweaters, and they did not notice Frank Tower moving down the back path behind the houses, toward his ultimate goal.

Two sweaters eased backward until he was flat on the ground; his head used the pavement as a pillow. He stretched out his arms and legs like a snow angel on the hard ground.

Nat shook his head. "I can't believe this. I don't want to get anywhere near this guy." He turned to the others. "Move him out."

Big man frowned. "I'm not touching that guy." His partner, the silent one, started to get back into the SUV.

"We could run him over." Nat looked down at his hip and exposed the handle of a weapon.

Big man warned, "That's too much police involvement. We don't need this." The large man also made a retreat to the vehicle.

On the ground, two sweaters swept his arms and legs, completing the movements of a snow angel. Then he started to say the same words over and over, louder each time. "I want to pee!"

"Dammit." Nat made a move to kick the man on the ground, only to be stopped by the big man who came running from the SUV. "You got too much on your tab right now with the police."

Nat just stood there, like someone trying to figure out the next move. "He'll move soon. The sun is gonna bake him."

Inside the house, all seven occupants were huddled against the windows watching the events going on yards away. They did not hear someone enter through the rear door.

"Hello." Frank Tower stood in the shadows of the kitchen.

A woman wearing jeans and a sweatshirt was the first to turn around. "Who are you?"

"My name is Frank Tower. Jackie sent me. If you all listen to me, we're going to get you out of here. I need you all to move away from the window. We don't want them thinking you're talking to someone."

The woman in jeans snapped at Tower, "Did you bring any food with you?"

"Food?"

"Yeah, food. These fools gave us two burgers to split seven ways. We're starving." She rolled her eyes at the ceiling. "Anyone even taking a step to escape dies."

As a group, they all walked to positions in the living room and near the kitchen. Tower took a quick look around. To his left, there were two bags on a table. One bag was ripped and Tower saw what looked like illegal drugs. Two bedrooms had bedding all over the place. Several sheets were stretched out on the floor. On his right, another two bedrooms, and again the unkempt beds.

"We don't have much time." Tower kept his voice calm and low. "Have they made any recent demands?"

Another woman spoke up. She was also wearing jeans. "They call me Streaker. I used to work the streets along with T.T. and Anna." She pointed to two others. "None of us want any police. Thanks to Jackie, we're trying to come off the drugs. And if we do that, we won't need to hook. At least, that's the plan."

Tower kept waving them away from the window. "Who is the businessman?"

"It's me," said a man wearing a blue button-down shirt and cargo shorts. "My company thinks I'm on vacation. I'm kicking pills."

Tower directed the women toward the rear door. "We don't have a lot of time. You're going to go out one at a time. Move right down the path like I did. Keep going. Please make sure they don't see you. When you get out to the connecting street, make a left. You'll see Jackie waiting for you with the rehab van. Mr. Businessman, I need you to keep walking in front of the window like you're all here. Is that clear?"

"Clear."

Tower looked inside the torn bag. Streaker pointed to it. There were small vials of cocaine, pills, and three nice mounds of black tar heroin. Streaker sniffed at the bag. "Enough temptation to get a whole city high. Coke, pills, you name it, it's in that bag. They want us on drugs again."

T.T. stared into Tower's face, then toward the bag. "You know how hard it is to stay away from this? They are counting on us to get weak and start using."

"Yeah," Streaker said, "no food, just drugs. Nothing till we're on the feed again. We're not doing it."

"Everyone ready?" They all nodded.

Streaker was the first to go. Tower walked with her to the edge of the house. In the street, two sweaters was standing and pretending to touch the car, then ran back away from the largest one. Tower whispered, "I know about Nat. Who are the other ones?"

She tried hard not to point. "The big guy, that's Duncan. All I know is everyone calls him Duncan. He's the enforcer. The other one is Darvis Kizner. He's quiet but he'll put a hurt'n on you if you owe Nat money."

"Thanks." When the moment was right, Tower sent Streaker running down the path. She paused at each house, then took off again until she was far off and down Tella.

The woman named T.T. was next. "We put the men on one side of the house, women on the other. I think one more day and I'd be on drugs again." She was faster than Streaker. Tower watched as she kicked up dust. Anna waited her turn and took off.

Tower looked inside the house. Businessman was still walking periodically in front of the window. Three men followed Tower's instructions, waiting for a cue, then ran toward safety. Only businessman remained.

Tower directed him outside. "Please tell everyone to leave. I'll take care of everything on this end."

"You sure?"

"Go."

Businessman took off. He wasn't as athletic as the others. Forty seconds later, he turned the corner and was out of sight. Tower looked out the window. Two sweaters was running around, moving away from the one they called Duncan. Tower took a moment and used his cell phone to photograph the three SUV occupants. He waited another ten minutes, then stepped outside, walking through the front door and into the street.

Kizner was the first to see someone other than the seven coming out of the house. He got Nat's attention. All three closed in around Tower.

They moved their attention away from Tower and on the bag of drugs he was holding. "Afternoon, gentlemen. Nasty stuff, drugs."

Nat's stare was lasered on Tower. "Where are my people?"

"Your people? You don't have any people, Nat. It's just you and the two idiots."

Nat gave an order to Kizner. "Go check inside." Kizner ran past Tower and went into the abandoned house. Tower took out the containers of coke and dumped them out, creating a drug puff that floated on the breeze and dissipated into nothing. He then spilled out the pills and crushed them with his shoes. Kizner ran out of the house. The run took most of the air from his lungs and his voice was shrill. "They're gone, Nat. There's no one in there."

"Where are they?" Nat demanded.

Tower did an extra few mashes of his right foot to make sure the pills were dust. "If you're upset, why don't you call the police? Tell them someone destroyed your drugs." Duncan started to move on Tower. Two sweaters shed both of the woolen coverings and showed the muscular arms of one Michael Thomas, private investigator. Tower pointed to him. "That's my friend. Black belt, weight-lifting champion, south district, former bouncer. I'd stay right where you are if I were you."

Duncan stopped his forward movement, all the while watching Thomas. Tower walked up to Nat, getting just two feet from him. "I want you to leave these people alone. If I hear you're messing with any of them or anyone wanting to get into rehab, you'll have to answer to me."

Nat's arms were lined with tattoos. There was a small cut on his forehead. "This is my house, my block. That's why no one came to help them. They know I run it." With each few words, his voice increased in volume. "You gotta pay for the stuff you destroyed."

"Pay for drugs? Not gonna happen. Here's what you have to understand, Nat. From this day on, you don't run anything. I'm going to make it my personal mission to make sure I toilet flush every drug you bring in here. And if you don't move off, I'll flush you."

Nat stood there. He closed all the fingers in his right hand and started to take a swing. Tower was anticipating a strike and blocked the swing as Nat's arm made the upward arc. Once the swing was blocked, it was Tower's turn to make a move. He thought of all the drug dealers who convinced Jackie crack was a far better choice than looking after her son. The missed meals, promises not kept, and all the times he tried to wake her from the dozed-out dream killer of the drug's effects. Every emotion and pure arm strength went into Tower's swing. When his fist crashed into Nat's face, the sound echoed off the windows in the four run-down houses in the cul-de-sac. Blood was spurting from Nat's mouth and his jaw disengaged from the rest of his face. The punch lifted Nat off his feet and sent him backward. Rage boiled in Tower's eyes, and it took his fellow P.I. to keep him from striking again. Nat's collapse on the ground sounded like a cow carcass being dumped on a killing floor.

Tower stood over him waiting for a return punch that did not come. Nat moaned as he blinked himself into consciousness. Duncan again leaned as if he was going to attack and yielded to the large man standing next to him.

Tower calmed down. There was still a fire of anger in him as though he weren't hitting just Nat, but every dealer that ever doled out poison.

Kizner got Nat to sit up and offered him a handkerchief that Nat refused. He was spitting blood. Duncan pulled him up and got Nat inside the SUV. Tower closed the door. "Remember, no reprisals. Got it?"

Tower snapped the door open again. In the corner of the SUV, he saw something on the rear seat. A jacket. For Tower, the material of the jacket exactly matched the material he found on the fence in Janine Iwan's gate. "Whose jacket is that?" When he didn't hear a response, he yelled the question a second time. "The jacket?"

Kizner mouthed, "Sta..."

The door slammed shut and the SUV drove off, blasting small rocks in all directions. Tower turned to his friend. "Thanks, man. I appreciate it."

"No problem." They both watched the SUV turn a corner and go out of sight.

"He started to say Stan." Tower rubbed his right fist. "Like Stan Brady."

25

Tower drove through the downtown district. On the street, the crowds of people were missing. The small park located in the middle of the district was empty. From his car, he saw stores had few customers. Parking lots were less than half full. He pulled into a space and walked into Ray's Restaurant.

After years of preparing delicacies of Ray's version of mac and cheese, peach cobbler, and steaks cooked on an indoor grill, the succulent aromas were literally baked into the walls of the place. Tower entered and smelled fried chicken. The restaurant had just one couple eating in the rear corner. Tower heard talk coming from the kitchen and two male voices in disagreement. There were loud scraping sounds of a smashed plate being swept up.

Ray himself approached Tower with an order pad. "Hello, Frank. What can I get you?"

"You cooking and waiting on tables? That's new." Tower did not need a menu.

The normal smile was gone from Ray's face. "People are scared. You got folks being snatched from their homes. It's not good, Frank. Business so bad, I told all the waitresses to go home."

"I just want some of your meatloaf to go. And some broccoli."

Ray wrote it all down. "My cook bumped into my clean-up man. Three dishes became history. Then an argument on who was gonna clean it up."

The maintenance man emerged from the kitchen with a bag. He emptied two small trash cans into the bag and went back into the kitchen, probably headed to the back door.

"Your guy okay after the spill with Brady?"

"Stacker? Yeah, he's fine. Nothing broken. The guy works hard. Let me get you that meatloaf." Ray stepped away, opening the kitchen door. Tower saw the busy hands of the cook. He was a stocky man with big arms and hair on his neck. Ray called over the clean-up man.

"Hey, Stacker."

He walked over, carrying a broom. Stacker was bald and turned his head to the side as if he was shy. He was lean like he could use a meal or two.

Ray sized him up. "Stacker, you okay? You took a bad fall."

"I'm fine." He looked at the floor again. "Can I go? Got a spill to clean up in the storage room."

"No problem. Take care." Stacker left.

Tower's eyes then settled on the outside. He sat next to a large window. The sun was dropping and the shadows were getting longer. Tower got his meal in less than fifteen minutes. He was not prepared to eat right away, so he dropped by his office, put the meatloaf in the fridge, and got back into his car.

Tower spent close to two hours circling around the Never Too Late and the now empty house on Tella Avenue. No signs of Nat or his thugs. By seven p.m., Tower unlocked the door to his office and decided to set up there for the night. After enjoying the meal, he took a needed shower and nestled in front of his computer. He made up profiles of Nat, Duncan, and Kizner, checking their arrest records and any information he could muster. Again, Tower was trying to connect a lot of dots. He couldn't figure out the direct connection between Nat and Stan Brady. The two were never arrested together, yet the jacket or arrest record was convincing.

Once the files were completed and saved by computer, Tower also kept the information on his phone, including past booking photos. He stopped and looked at a picture of Shannon. He missed the questions from her about clients and what cases he was working. Tower no longer thought she was probing, trying to find out if there was a clandestine meeting with another woman.

Tower's actions a few years earlier almost crushed the marriage. The affair with a client lasted just months, yet left emotions raw. He saw the look on her face of whether she could ever trust him again. Every day since, he had done what he could to repair the trust.

There was a knock at the door.

T.O. was disheveled. Her hair needed attention and her shoes were different colors. "I can't sleep."

"C'mon in."

Her small frame made a loud sound as she dropped on the couch in the office. Tower pulled up a chair and sat in front of his desk. "Thinking about Preston?"

"Every day." She started punching the couch leather. "At least I'm not throwing glasses."

"No bars?"

"Not a drop. Sober as the reverend's wife."

"I'm guessing you want an update?"

"I just want to talk to someone. My roommate's boyfriend is over and my conversations about Pres just bring everybody down. So, I thought I'd come here."

Tower poured them both a glass of water. He could not tell her about the countdown clock. Not yet. "You already know about Stan Brady. They're looking for him. Ever heard of him?"

She eased her body down to the right side so her face was on the couch and looked at Tower from an angle. "I must have looked at his mug a thousand times. Nothing." She sat up again. "The police saying anything?"

"Not much. Just what's been on the news." Tower looked away from her for a second, concerned she might see through him. He was mostly telling the truth. There was so much that had to remain between him and Mark

David. "I'm going to check a few places in the morning where Brady was last seen. I just can't get in the way of the police."

T.O. put her head down again, and one eye closed. She got up. "Bathroom?"

Tower pointed in the direction of the restroom when his phone rang. "Hello, Shannon."

She sounded energetic. "Can't wait to see you. Anything new?"

"Not a lot." He brought her up to speed on what he could share and then there was a flushing noise.

"Are you home?"

Tower thought about how he could honestly answer the question. "I'm at the office."

T.O. approached him. "Frank, can I sleep on the couch? It's late."

Shannon's words were crisp. "Who is that?"

"It's a cli-"

"A client?" Now her question was on fire. "Another client? Really, Frank?"

"Her name is T.O. Her friend was murdered. I'm looking into the case. You can meet her when you arrive."

Behind him, T.O. was again punching up a soft spot in the couch to put her head. Tower pushed the phone up tight against his mouth. "I don't want to use the T word here, but you've got to trust me. She just came over for an update. I'll let her sleep on the couch and I'll be in the van. I swear. I can FaceTime you if you want."

Thirty, forty seconds went by. Long enough for a marriage to again implode or build a stronger bridge. As he waited, Tower went to a closet for a blanket. "Call me back, Shannon. Give me five minutes and you'll see my sleeping arrangements. I'll be like a monk."

"I'll see you when I see you." Conversation over. By the time Tower eased the blanket over T.O., she was out. He grabbed the van keys, locked the front door, pulled the van out of the garage, and parked in front. He rolled the windows down one-third and pulled down a cot he had mounted into the van's roof. Tower tried to sleep, but it was hard. He kept thinking about the whereabouts of Stan Brady and what he might be doing.

In the morning, Tower kept away the glare of sunlight by using all the black-out material in the van. He turned on his police scanner and listened as he rubbed sore muscles from sleeping on the cot. He heard what he feared most. There was a hard knock on the driver's side window. T.O. tried to look into the van. Tower parted the curtain, still wearing his clothes from last night.

There was a panicked look on T.O.'s face. "They found another one."

26

Tower never got used to the smell of death.

T.O. left for her apartment and Tower drove to what the locals of Stilton Bay called Little Everglades. Quiet Streams Park was a seventeen-acre gift of nature. Tall oak trees and palmetto palms inhabited the place. A part of the park nestled up to the Intracoastal Waterway, and was lined by mangroves. The waterway eventually led to the ocean.

As soon as Tower got out of the car, he took it all in. The ocean air was taken over by the stench of human rot. The entire parking lot was blocked off by crime tape, and Tower parked a few car spaces from the entrance to Quiet Streams. With each step, the odor was building. Stay at a crime scene too long and the putrid air got into your clothes, your very pores, and it would take an hour-long shower to wash it out. He mentally blocked out the rancid air and kept walking until he reached three police officers standing near the crime tape.

One of them spoke before Tower said a word. "You Frank Tower? Just show me some I.D. and we'll take you in."

Tower was surprised. "You want me inside?"

"Just following orders. Your I.D., sir."

Tower pulled out his driver's license and flashed the plastic at the officer. "Follow me."

He pulled up the tape and Tower ducked under. A TV crew was far off to the right. Just a handful of onlookers. Tower made sure he followed exactly in the steps taken by the officer since this was a crime scene. He was led to a cluster of detectives. Tower knew all of them. Mark David made his way through the pack and approached Tower. "Not gonna lie, you're here in case this person is watching. I wanted to make sure it looked like we're keeping you in the loop."

Tower said, "I know you have a vic. Can you say much?"

"To you, officially, nothing. As I told you before, I will only tell you what will go into the press release. In case this guy is out here somewhere taking pictures, I want you prominent and in front."

"Even if that's not true."

"Play along with me, Frank. Here's the deal." Mark David pulled out his notepad. "On the record, we're not releasing any possible names until we notify next of kin. I can tell you it's a male, somewhere in his sixties. We do have a missing persons report that was filed late last night. And we have recovered a burned-out SUV that we think belongs to the victim."

Jake May walked near Tower, then stopped. "If Brady is responsible for this and you let him go, I'll make sure this haunts you for the rest of your life."

"I didn't let anyone go. You had him in your net. He got away from you, not me."

Jake May moved on.

Tower was just about to ask where the victim was located in the park when his eyes drifted to a well-worn pathway. There were two paths in the park and each one had its own name.

The body was positioned near the White Lily path. Tower saw a man strapped next to the sign. He was wearing a hiker's hat, shorts, a short-sleeve fishing shirt, and no shoes. Tower could only see him from the side and guessed his eyes must be open. The real Everglades were almost fourteen miles west of Stilton Bay in Broward County. This tiny version was home to birds, the usual array of South Florida animals, and an occasional buzzard. Tower noticed an officer dabbing on more Vicks under his nose to mask the smell. The killer made it look like the victim was walking in the park, taking in the view. A stream S-curved through the heart of the park and there were white everglades lilies in the green-black water. Tower knew this was a popular spot for teenagers looking for a make-out location. They usually parked in the lot.

"We failed." Mark David slapped the notepad against his right leg. "You're right. It was on us to find Brady. He's still out there and now we have this."

"You sure it's Brady?" Tower repeated his doubt.

"You back on that?"

Tower pulled out his phone and tapped. "I just sent you an email. Never say I didn't give you anything. It implicates Brady more than anything."

David looked at his phone. Several minutes into his reading of the information from Tower, he shot a question. "When did this happen?"

"Yesterday. It's all in there. I had a confrontation with three guys. The names are in there. They were hassling some people."

"Some people?"

"I'm not going to get into all the details unless I have to, but yeah, it was them and me. The bottom line is there was a jacket in the back seat. Did you get that cloth sample I told your folks about?"

"We got it."

"Well, if you catch up to these mugs, they had a jacket in the back of the car, and I can't swear to it, but I think the jacket belongs to Brady."

"So, these guys might be running with him?"

"That's my guess. But I still don't make him for these murders."

Mark David tapped on his phone. "I'm sending this to my team. We'll get an A.P.B. out on these guys." He looked hard at Tower. "Anything else you want to tell me?"

"Not right now."

The tiny bit of sharing information was for Mark David. And only him. Tower's time on the force was pleasant in parts because of David. The time they spent together in the street when they were both in uniform remained the strong tie that bound them together. A relationship that grayed the line as far as sharing facts. Mark David could tell him very little and Tower had to protect his clients. Both tried to limit what they exchanged as a defense attorney would tear apart the practice.

Tower tried to avoid asking Mark David if they found a thumb drive.

The crime scene techs were busy taking photographs of the victim. There were a few cones placed on the ground, marking the locations of possible evidence. By the smell, Tower guessed he was in the park for two days. The Florida heat and daily humidity would ramp up the body gases. Tower was just glad they got to him before he started to bloat. The body was too far away to see if the maggots had started.

The countdown clock went to zero and detectives were not able to save the third victim.

For the next hour, Tower watched Mark David's team work the scene. Then, one tech, after taking dozens of photographs of the victim's right hand, pulled something from the almost closed fist. The item was bagged and handed over to Mark David. For Tower, the item had to be the thumb drive. Another clock, another victim was in the future. Tower, the team, the entire force had to do something. And now.

Tower dealt with a series of facts. Three victims and all of them were staged to look like they were enjoying life. All were in favorite places for the public: a pond for ducks, the fishing pier, and now a walk in Quiet Streams Park. Were these all places important to the victims or the killer? The hard reality was simply these crime locations were now a point of morbid curiosity for some and outright frightening for others who no longer ventured to the city's great landmarks.

Sixteen minutes passed and Tower got the attention of Mark David, letting him know he was about to leave. He nodded and Tower walked with an officer back to the crime tape line. Once outside the confines of the investigation field, Tower headed for his car.

"Frank! Frank Tower." The call came from his left. Tower recognized the voice. Attorney Stu Baker waved his hands to get his attention. Tower went to him. "Stu. I think it's been a year since I saw you. You still doing defense work?"

"Till they take my law books away." Baker was always dressed to the max. Two-thousand-dollar suit, white shirt with a gray-and-blue striped tie and matching cuffs. His shoes were buffed to a high shine and sweat would not dare linger on his face. "I'm trying to get someone's attention, but I don't know, maybe the police are not too happy to see me here. I've had three successful not guilty verdicts in the past eighteen months."

"Stu, why are you here?"

"I'm not sure yet, but I think I know the victim."

27

Tower made sure their conversation was not overheard. "What makes you say that?"

"Ro was supposed to, well, let me start over. Roland Kincade was going to meet me for some legal matters but he never showed. I didn't give it much thought. He changes his mind all the time. I drove past his house and did not see his SUV. Then, I heard on the news about a man being found in the woods, so I came over."

"You're an attorney. You know how things work. I'm going to direct you to the lead detective. If you want, once you speak with him, I'd also like to ask you some questions."

The answer did not come right away. Tower reasoned his attorney mind was processing everything before he spoke. "I can do that. Show me where to go."

Tower led him to the police tape and spoke with the officer. After a short radio conversation, Baker was taken to an area where a tent was set up.

No matter how long, Tower was prepared to wait for Baker. As he looked around the crowd, Tower noticed one or two members of the Stilton Bay Police force in street clothes. A good idea, Tower thought. Put some of your people with the onlookers and you catch a killer coming back to gawk.

Twenty minutes after he went inside the police tape, Baker came back. The usually stoic and unfazed look of a veteran court lawyer was now drawn. His eyes focused on the ground, never looking into the faces of the few people still remaining. The collar was unbuttoned and the tie was loose, almost an afterthought. His shoes were a dusty mess with leaves stuck to one heel. Baker was not his normal court-ready self. He drove his hands through his hair, messing up the once perfect coif. He didn't look up until he reached Tower.

"They wouldn't let me get too close. But I'm sure it's him. They said some I.D. was left in his pocket."

"What does that tell you?"

"It says the killer wants police to know who this is, no question." Both men stopped when they were in an area with no one around. "I owe you one, Frank. Years ago, you found a vital witness for me. That witness produced a not guilty verdict. My guy couldn't find him but you did. You said you had some questions?"

"Yes. Would Kincade have any contact or knowledge of a Preston Wakefield?"

Baker shook his head. "No. I don't think so."

"What about Saneele Gunson?"

"No, that name does not sound familiar. Are they victims?"

"Yes. Both killed in the same manner. So your guy Kincade, was he still working?"

"Heck no. He sold his business years ago. He had no money worries. No kids. Wife divorced him, then she passed away so long ago I can't remember."

"What did he do now?"

"All I know is he loved his house. Had the biggest fireplace in South Florida. Could only use it twice a year." Baker let out a hollow laugh.

"You say you went by his place. You see anything irregular?"

"No. He was about to get a dog, I remember that. He had a few health issues, but he was doing fine."

"What did the police tell you to do?"

"I might have to identify him but that will come later. If you don't mind,

I don't want to see them move him out of here. Mind if we go somewhere else?"

"Stu, if you got time, I'd like to go back to the house."

"I'll meet you there."

The drive took fifteen minutes. Tower had parked his car next to a crime scene van. Crews were already inside the house. Every now and then Tower saw the flash from their cameras.

On the drive to Kincade's house, Tower went over every possible connection to the two earlier victims. So far, no one was able to draw a line linking all three. When Baker got out of the car, the suit coat and dress shirt were gone, replaced by a polo. Baker, a man who had been to easily a hundred crime scenes as a defense attorney, was clearly shaken by the swirl of people going over the home of Roland Kincade.

There were people in the backyard, carefully moving through the grass, looking for any speck of evidence. Kincade's home was in the Palm Branch Gardens section of the city. All of the lots were one or two acres, packed with palm trees and rock landscaping. The front yard had a nice stack of cut wood. Another cord was placed neatly against the wall. From outside, an impressive build-up of rock formed the main shape of a chimney. All indications hinted the inside would be just as impressive.

"I just got a text. They want to take me around in there, see if I can spot anything missing or not right."

Tower said, "You up for that?"

"If this is him, if he is the next victim, then yes, I'd do anything to find the bastard who killed him."

"Let me ask, was Roland a beer drinker?"

"Ro? Heck no. He got a heart scare once or twice. Gave up beer and wine. He liked to chop wood for exercise."

"I hate to put it this way, but did he keep his place neat? Or manly dirty."

"Clean, everything put away. You wouldn't find that in my house."

"Stu, another favor. When they take you in there, take a good look at the tabletops, the countertops and see if there are any dried circle rings. Like someone was resting a beer there."

"In Ro's place? I don't think I'll find it but I'll look."

Three minutes later, Mark David arrived. His face was serious. Three victims and no suspects would do that to a detective. He waved Stu Baker over. David, Baker, and Jake May all went inside. All three men put on body gear so they would not contaminate the inside. Coverings also went on their feet. As they entered, David pointed to the ground as if to show him where he could walk.

Tower stood in the shade of an oak tree. He checked his phone for any messages. There were two, both from T.O. She knew about the latest victim but had no details and wanted to talk. Tower texted he would make it to her in the afternoon. A trip to his car yielded a bottle of water. In thirty minutes of watching, the crime techs walked out with three dozen bags of evidence. Baker finally came out of the house. He made a direct path for Tower.

"They told me not to tell you anything."

"Stu, all I'm doing is trying to fill in the blanks, which can help with the investigation. That's all."

"I didn't say I'd agree to that request. I just listened."

Tower offered his theory. "I think the killer takes his time and sits down and takes a drink of some sort. He is purposely taking all the time he needs to enjoy a beverage, probably a beer. He does all this as part of his ritual. Why? I'm not sure yet. I just know it's the same pattern now, three times."

The attorney stepped forward so he was completely in the shade. He looked at the house. "We had some great parties in there. Place could hold a hundred people. The world just lost a great guy."

Tower said, "And the inside?"

"You were right. Circle rings of something on the coffee table. I pointed it out to Mark David. He acted like it was nothing."

"Part of his job."

"What's the deal on the rings? Ro start drinking again?"

"I'm not sure. Where are you headed?"

"To the morgue. They're moving on this fast. I'm about the only one who can identify him in a quick fashion."

"Sorry about Ro."

"Let me tell you something. Many years ago, just after I got my driver's license, like any teen, I went looking for a car. I found this beautiful two-door Ford. White, with painted black rims. I loved the thing. I put down the money and got ready to drive it off the lot. Just one problem. The Ford was a stick shift on the column. I didn't know how to drive a stick. First, I was embarrassed about it so I didn't want to give the car back to the dealer. I sat there trying to figure out how to get this car home. So, I went into the office and called Ro. Someone dropped him off and Ro met me at the car. He knew how to drive a stick and he drove that Ford to my house. Over the next two days, he taught me how to drive a stick shift. Now that, Frank Tower, is a true friend."

"Nice story."

Stu rubbed his right eye. "Was a good friend. Shows you the type of guy he was. I miss him. This is a terrible day. The thing is, from now on, all the days will be terrible."

28

Tower drove toward T.O.'s apartment building with the comfort of cruising the streets. His streets. All the days and nights on road patrol were almost therapy. The situations didn't matter. He broke up disputes between hookers, answered domestic calls, and tried to bring calm to arguments that clearly belonged in civil court. The streets, especially at night, received all the bad behavior possible with drunks heaving, an occasional blood-letting from a knife fight, or the tears of a victim's family. The streets took it all in until Mother Nature washed it all away, and in the morning, a searing sun dried up the roads and sidewalks, giving everything a clean slate.

There was no need to rush, and Tower kept the car just above the speed limit.

His right front tire exploded. Tower heard the shot at the same time and knew this wasn't a normal blowout. Someone was shooting at him. He managed to get control of the car and did not want to stop or else risk becoming an easy target. The second shot hit the passenger door with a hard thud. Tower reached for his Glock. Now armed, Tower stayed in the car and looked for the shooter. He recognized the face.

Duncan.

If Duncan was on his right, one of his co-thugs had to be nearby. Tower checked the rearview mirror and off to his left. Nothing. Rather than stop and engage, Tower hit the gas pedal. It would be Duncan's choice to keep shooting at a moving target or chase.

Three blocks down the road, Tower pulled over. He was not hit. Seven police cars, lights, and sirens encircled him. Tower identified himself, showed his licenses, and told them where his legal Glock was in the car and got out. Hands up until they could check him out.

Tower explained all the circumstances and did whatever they instructed him to do. He got permission to walk around and examine the car.

Mark David drove up.

"I can't leave you for two minutes, Frank."

"Welcome."

"You know who it was?"

"Yep. His name on the street is Duncan. I sent you some information about him. Might be running with Brady."

"And why would this Duncan be so enamored with you?"

"Just my good looks."

"C'mon, Frank. I don't have time to watch over you. I would normally let road patrol handle this but it might have something to do with my case, so here I am."

Tower looked down at the blown tire and the hole in the side of his car. "This was a warning. If they really wanted to come after me, they would bring the heavy stuff. This was just saying hello."

"Again, Frank, what's going on? There is a lot you're not telling me."

"Okay. I'll be honest with you. You be honest with me."

Three of the police cars drove off. A few seconds later, another three left. One car and one uniform stayed.

"I got crime techs coming. As if they don't have enough to do. So, what is it, Frank? Why are they after you?"

Tower hesitated. "Certain things I don't want in a report."

"Okay. I want to know it all. Everything. When the sergeant gets here, you tell him what you want. I'm not telling you to leave out something when you talk to him."

"Fine. I told you about Nat and his two friends. They run the drugs all around the Never Too Late. Some of his best customers gave it all up and they started rehab."

"Your mother's place."

"You mean Jackie's place. In order to convince them to start using again, he corralled them in a house, offered up bags of free drugs, and waited to get them hooked again. But he wouldn't let them leave."

"Nice."

"Exactly. Well, I broke up the party. Got them out and they are all back in rehab. So Nat is not too happy with me." Tower dared to ask a question. "I know you can't tell me anything, but did your guys do or find anything regarding the water rings on the countertop?"

"You heard about all that?"

"Yeah."

"Well, the crime techs didn't do much with it. The problem is some circle rings on a counter can't and probably won't lead them to an individual. Because of that, they took some pictures but that was about it. They're just water marks."

"Marks found at all three places. There has to be more to it."

"My crime techs don't think so. I don't know what to tell you, Frank. That's just their thinking."

"And what about you?"

"I've known you long enough to know that a possible piece of evidence that you spotted is more than likely a concrete lead. It's something that's on the table with my guys. But again, if this doesn't help them identify a person, they don't get too excited by it."

"Got it."

"On these thugs, you need some help from us?"

"I can handle it."

"You sure?"

"I got this. You've got too much going on right now; the least I can do is work out my own problems."

"Okay. But if you need me."

"I know. I know. Get out of here, Mark."

Mark David drove off in his all-black Dodge Durango Pursuit. Tower called his insurance company but told them he would take care of the damages himself. A crime tech took about thirty pictures. Tower took his own set of photographs. He also walked up to the spot where Duncan was shooting. No brass left behind and no cigarette butts.

Two hours later, after a talk with the sergeant and some angry looks from drivers who had to slow down, Tower changed the damaged tire and was moving again.

A hard adrenalin was flowing through him, giving purpose to his firm grip on the steering wheel. Nat just moved to the top of the list of slime that needed to be removed from the streets of Stilton Bay before the next rain and the rising sphere of the sun in the morning.

29

Tower had two stops to make. T.O. met him downstairs from her apartment. Before he got a chance to get out of the car, she ran to him, arms outstretched, and hugged him tight. He was surprised by the grip, and rather than loosen, she kept a firm hold of him. She rested her head on his chest. Tower tapped her arm as a sign she could let go. She did not. For Tower, T.O. was moving past a marker he set for himself after the affair. He didn't want a client to get that close again.

When he moved to free himself of the clutch, she held on. "You can let go. Or should I say, time out."

Her eyes came up to meet his and she gave him a T.O. smile. "Are you okay? I heard they were shooting at you."

He firmly broke free and moved back two feet. "I'm fine. Comes with the job."

"I was worried about you."

"I wanted to bring something up. You don't have to stay on as a client. I can update you on what I find, but you don't have to pay me."

"You mean end this?"

"By end this, if you mean the P.I.-client arrangement, then yes, you can move on and I promise to keep you apprised of what I find out."

"What if I don't want to end the arrangement?" The right side of her mouth bent downward in a half smile as if teasing him.

"I think I've got you a good start on information. The police are handling this far better than I could right now."

"I don't think so. Another person was killed and they still don't have a clue."

"They are working a lot of leads."

"What can you tell me? Like what?"

"There's certain things I can't pass on. Things only the killer would know. Let me ask you this, you think Preston knew a Roland Kincade?"

"Kincade? I don't think so. Never heard that name."

"I already asked you about Gunson."

"Yeah, nothing clicks. Who is Kincade anyway?"

"Just keep that name to yourself for now."

She looked beyond the parking lot, toward the downtown district. "Everyone is petrified. I mean this guy is taking who he wants, when he wants. And not one person has been able to stop him." T.O. remained in the sizzle of the heat rather than find shade. Her forehead was dotted with sweat. "I try not to think about Pres too much. If I do, I go into a downward spiral. I can't do that. Pres wouldn't like it."

"Can you think of any reason why the photograph was taken from Preston's apartment?"

"No. I keep trying to figure it out, but I can't."

"Promise me, if you think of anything, please let me know."

"Promise."

Tower backed up to the driver's side and got in. He lowered the window. "And be careful."

She went around to the passenger side of the car. "Look at that hole. You know who did it?"

"Take care. I'll call later."

～

Tower drove west into T-Town and stopped in the back row of the Never Too Late's parking lot. He wanted the bullet side of the car as far away from the door as possible. He didn't want to invite another question about what happened. Jackie was already out the door, moving fast to meet him.

"Guess you heard too?" Tower always stayed outside.

"Word moves fast around here. You okay?" She looked him up and down. "I worry about you."

"I'm fine. I just stopped to see if you're okay."

"I'm okay. But better than that, my people are safe. I can't thank you enough, Frankie, for what you did."

"Did Nat or his boys come by here?"

"Here? No. I will tell you this, police units have been by, making rounds. Good to see."

Behind Jackie, seven people walked out the front door. They no longer had that spellbound look of addiction. Once they reached Jackie, they stopped. Businessman spoke for the group. "We just wanted to thank you for what you did for us. We really had no gumption to fight Nat. We thank you."

Tower nodded. "The thank you goes to you for staying in the program. You all had the chance to take an easy path and take drugs again but you didn't. I applaud that. And a lot of the thanks goes to Jackie. From what I hear, this is a great program."

One of the former hookers tugged on what looked like a new skirt. "Through Jackie and the courts, we actually have jobs lined up. We can't thank her enough, but also you rescued us. We don't want to go back to the old life again. We just wanted to come out and say that."

"You're welcome."

They turned and walked back inside.

Jackie blinked a few times. "Either the sun got in my eye or I need new glasses."

"Listen, if Nat or any of his idiots come here, call me immediately. Is that clear?"

"Clear. How is your client? What's her name?"

"She calls herself T.O. She's a bit impulsive, but she's okay. We're still trying to figure out who is behind the killings." Tower walked back to his car. He almost said the M word. The term Mom was still new to Tower, given she was never there for him. For now, she was a mother of sorts to people who needed a new direction in their lives. Not Tower.

When he got behind the wheel, Tower only thought of the police investigation and the discovery of another victim. Also, why Mark David never contacted him with another thumb drive message from the killer.

30

Jake May clicked a key on the computer and held his breath. May and Mark David sat waiting for the thumb drive file to open. They were both expecting another clock. Once opened, the message read:

THE TIME WILL COME

May read the words out loud. "Time will come. What does that mean?"

David wrote down the message. "It means we might have some time to find him before he does something. There are no other files, right?"

"Just the one."

Mark David leaned back in his chair. May used gloves to pull out the drive, carefully putting it back into the evidence bag. "Maybe he's done with his list."

"No way. I'm not going to bring Tower into this since he was not mentioned." He studied the drive. "And still no prints?"

"Crime techs say it's clean. Just like the others. And the places were clean. Kincade, Wakefield, Gunson, they all showed no prints. This guy obviously used gloves and maybe foot coverings while inside. He was careful not to touch much. The location of the burned-out van showed signs he used something to wipe up the tire tracks. Brush marks all over. He made sure where he went had no cameras. Homes, roads, the woods in the park. And no pictures."

"Just that blurry image outside a bar."

May went down his own list. "Nothing of note from the public. Two people confessed to the crimes and were quickly checked out as quacks. Another ten people or so are convinced this is the work of an alien being. No one so far has any credible information on what he looks like or if they saw anything. This guy is a ghost who travels in between the raindrops."

"Ghosts end up in jail. What's the latest on Brady?"

"Now, on him, we do have some information. He's been spotted a few times selling drugs in and around T-Town. We stepped up our patrols there. You already know about the Duncan shooting."

David said, "We have to find that guy and pin this down. I mean, we have his prints on file, DNA, everything. Brady doesn't seem like the type to be that cautious at a crime scene. He's a human scattergun of trace evidence."

David tapped his fingers on the table. He kept tapping until he came to an inner conclusion. "Why don't you send Sonia back and re-interview all the people who found the bodies. See if there is something we're missing. I just know we are close."

31

Janine Iwan tapped the microphone before she spoke. She stood between two large speakers from the P.A. system set up on the beach. Before her, some thirty people were spread out on the sand, squinting at the marvelous glare of a morning sunrise.

"I know how devastated you were to hear about Saneele Gunson, just like I was. I also know most of you called her "the plant lady." She didn't mind it. But I'm here to tell you she was much, much more than a person learned about plants."

The faces of those present were a wide collection of emotions. Anger among a few. Others were reflective, as if poring through multitudes of thoughts about Gunson. Still, in the faces of most, there was fear. A monster roamed the city, snatching souls with no end yet to the torment.

Behind the crowd, off to the side, was Frank Tower. He was there to support Iwan and he also wanted to people-watch. A quick pan from left to right showed a few of Mark David's team, in civis, blending in with the sea-grape trees. In Tower's reasoning, this would be a perfect time for someone to watch and revel in all the misery.

Iwan's voice started to crack. "We were so close growing up. And that friendship continued all these years. She would be so overjoyed to see all of you in a much happier moment, talking about plant cuttings or how to grow orchids. She only wanted to make things better in life. Someone took her from us but we must not ever forget the things she did for Stilton Bay. Saneele led the way to save the middle of the city for a park, rather than shops. I don't want to throw too much at the city, but they were planning on taking away everything green until Saneele stood up and protested. When she was done with that, she got plants installed all around the city."

Among the crowd, tears were falling like a soft Florida rain.

Tower roamed from his position, glancing up and checking out the buildings and the parking lot for any late arrivals. Already, Tower heard of calls being made to the mayor's office to rename a park in honor of Gunson.

On the makeshift podium, speakers were taking turns talking about her. The beachside memorial was probably something Gunson would have liked. Overhead, seagulls drifted on the slipstreams over the water and landed on the nearby pier. Ten more speakers gave short speeches until Iwan again stepped before the microphone to wrap the service.

"The best way to honor her is to do something she would like. There are beach clean-ups four times a year. You could volunteer at the Nature Center. Just remember to treat yourself to a great day. Thanks for coming out."

Tower walked to the podium, which consisted of a rug stretched out on the beach, a small generator to power the P.A. system, and rows of plants. Tower had to move out of the way of the two guys putting away the equipment. "I forgot she did all that for the city."

Iwan didn't fight the wind and let the air blow her strands around. "She was a special lady."

Tower stood, looking out at the thinning crowd, and something got his attention. "Excuse me." He looked left and right a few times to again fix his sight on a flashing object. He found it. The object was in a palm tree about ten feet up. When he reached the tree, Tower knew exactly what was there.

A wireless surveillance camera.

His immediate urge was to pull it down. He repressed it since he knew the thing might be evidence. The next move was a phone call.

"Mark. It's Frank. I'm down here at the beach for the Gunson memorial. If your people are still here, I found a surveillance camera. Wireless."

Tower got off the phone and waited. He was joined by Janine Iwan. "What is that?"

"Don't worry about it. I've got police on the way. I think someone wanted to watch the memorial from a distance."

Iwan's face moved from glum to worried. "Watching us?"

"Maybe. We don't know yet. You did fine. Saneele would be proud."

"I better make sure everything is put away." She trudged through the sand back to the flowers.

Big Jake May got out of his unmarked. Behind him was a crime tech, who brought a ladder. The tech took at least a dozen photographs before setting up the ladder, then once he got closer, he took another dozen photos.

Tower was joined by May. "Good eye, Frank."

"If this is your guy, he could be watching through an app and be anywhere in the world."

May held the ladder steady. "We'll check it for DNA, prints, the gamut."

Both men watched as the tech, wearing gloves, plucked the camera out of the crook of the tree and held it up to the light. The camera was small.

"How in the world did you see that thing?" Jake kept holding the ladder as the tech stepped down.

"I saw the sun flashing on something. And it didn't look natural. I moved in closer and found the camera."

"Many thanks."

"If you don't mind, I'm going to drive up A1A and look around. If I see something, I'll give you a call."

"Just don't touch anything, Frank."

Tower got into his car and drove toward the business district, all the time keeping his eyes on drivers coming from the opposite direction. He had no idea what this guy might look like and he just wasn't convinced Brady was tech savvy. He made four trips up and down the roads near the pier and the beach. Tower slapped his right thigh hard. He forgot to ask May if there was another thumb drive message.

Four phone calls to Mark David all went to voicemail. He gave up. Tower decided he would spend the day looking for one Stan Brady.

32

Tower sat parked in front of the house for twenty minutes before knocking on the door. A smiling woman with slender hips answered the door. "Are you police too?"

"My name is Frank Tower, Private Investigator."

"You ain't as cute as that Dee-teck-dive David, but you'll do. You want to come in?"

"Oh no, I'll stay right here."

She was wearing jeans cut so high and short, the pockets protruded. Her tall brown legs gave her a model's body. The proverbial last thing Tower wanted to do would be to step into a closed-door environment with her. "Afraid to come in, huh?"

"I know Stan is not here, but I have a message for him."

"Just who is Stan?" She opened the door wider.

"Your boyfriend, Stan. Stan Brady."

"I'm not dating anyone, honey. You bring me some flowers and ask real nice, maybe I can see what you're made of."

The task would not be easy, yet Tower tried to scope out the house as fast as he could without her knowing what he was doing. A wall blocked off half the house and a trail of crumbs indicated where the TV viewing was done. Off to the left was a dining room now filled with boxes of all sizes.

Down the hallway straight ahead was the kitchen, and Tower was clearly able to see the stacks of unwashed dishes on the table and in the sink.

"I just have a message for Stan, that is, if you see or hear from him."

She sarcastically said, "Who?"

"Just tell him Frank Tower said I don't think he hurt anyone."

"I've been telling the police that. Stan wouldn't do anything to anyone."

It was Tower's turn. "Who?"

She laughed. "You got me."

He handed her a business card. "Just tell him what I said. And if he wants to turn himself in, I'll go with him to the police department."

"Wait, your name is Tower. Frank Tower, as in the guy who investigated Stan for workman's comp? That Tower? Why are you even at my door? You piece-a-sh-"

Tower cut her off. "I know. I know. Yeah, I'm that guy. What he was doing was wrong. And he knows it. I also think the police have him pegged for something he did not do. Stan is a lot of things, but killer, I don't think so. Just tell him what I said."

"I'll think about it." The door slammed so hard Tower thought the screws would fall out of the frame.

Four cars pulled up in the street. Tower turned to see Mark David get out of his car. What Tower did not realize was both sides of the house were surrounded by members of S.W.A.T. Jake May also got out of a car. Two uniforms stood by, waiting for instructions. The S.W.A.T. leader motioned to Tower to move back from the door.

Tower knew all this attention and personnel could only mean one thing: a search warrant.

Mark David waited.

The team leader knocked and talked at the same time. "Stilton Bay Police. Open the door."

Seconds later, she was back at the door. The presence of so many police did not faze her. "I'm Miss Popularity today. What is it?"

The team leader looked past her and into the house, then turned to Mark David and gave an all-clear signal. David approached. "We have a warrant to search the house." He handed her the paperwork. "Please go with this uniformed officer while we conduct the search." A tall officer approached her and she moved away from the door without any comment. Tower remembered, like a lot of departments, Stilton Bay always carried out search warrants with S.W.A.T. in the lead.

Tower was allowed to go back to his car. He watched a crime tech team arrive in a white van. They wore full body coverings and went into the house with a stack of empty evidence bags. Forty-five minutes later, they started a trail to the van with bags of various sizes. From what Tower could see, there were no weapons, not even a computer. The comings and goings from the house took almost two hours before they were finished. Mark David left. Police cars pulled away. Only she and Tower remained.

She looked at him and let her emotions pour out through her eyes. Two brown spheres turning to fire. She pulled out Tower's business card and tore it into tiny pieces, then blew them out of her hand, watching them fall like snowflakes in the Florida sun. She continued to glare at Tower, her cheeks swelling with fluid, then she spat a huge glob in Tower's direction, her face etched in disgust.

33

More than anything, Tower was a bit hungry, even after watching her spit. A meal would have to wait. Attorney Stu Baker urged him to stop by his office. A man sitting at the reception desk waved Tower on, pointing to the large conference room. Baker was there, sitting in front of a wall of law books.

Tower sat down. Baker looked back at the book wall. "Funny thing. We never take those books out and look at them anymore. It's just for show. People like to see a lawyer with a bunch of books."

Tower was getting impatient. "Why did you call for me?"

Baker blew some dust off his mahogany desk. "I know they, I mean the police, told me not to say anything, but I feel I can still share a few things with you."

Tower sat back in the chair. "Go ahead."

"I thought about what you said. When I was looking around with the detectives, there were some things missing. All photographs. Pictures of a ski trip we took four years ago. A picture at one of our favorite restaurants. It was like someone was trying to steal memories."

"You tell the police?"

"Oh, yeah. And it's terrible because those were the only photographs from those trips. I always meant to get a copy. Never did."

"Stu, what does your gut tell you? What does the killer want?"

"Quite honestly, I don't know. Ro never uttered a bad word about anyone. What happened to him is going to stick with me the rest of my life. When your best friend dies, your whole life moves in another direction. And you think about it all the time."

Stu put his hand up to his face to prop up his head as he talked. Much different than the fiery brand of closing argument he was known for in the courtroom. Once Stu Baker spoke for almost three hours during a closing. He acted out the alleged crime, all the while explaining in detail why his client could not be the one who did the crime. On that day, Baker won. The man was freed. Now his words were soft and calm, like someone had attacked his inner being. Losing a friend would do that to a person.

"I want this man caught." Stu was standing now. "That's why I called for you. I don't care police told me to be quiet. I can't be quiet while his killer is out there. I've hired you before. My accountant can write you up a check. I want you to very discreetly find this person."

"Someone already hired me. I'm going to do this now for free. Too many people have been hurt. I'm going to find out something. I just need time."

Tower got up and left. There was nothing more to say. He got his car, and about twenty minutes later he was standing in front of T.O. She met him at Tower's office, rather than her apartment. Her way of keeping her roommate away from the conversation.

Tower could feel the heat coming off T.O.'s body. She was in angry mode again. "How far are you going to take this? The man who killed Preston is out there and you want to make it easier for him to get away with this?"

He thought of the words to say without causing her to reach for a glass to throw. "All they want is to question him, that's it. They carried out a search warrant to help rule him out."

"Just question him!" She shouted the words; her voice bounced around the room. The veins in her neck popped. She pointed her finger at Tower like a saber. "I paid you to find this beast, not let him walk. Do your job."

Tower kept a calm tone. "I'm looking for him. I want police to do whatever they need to find the right person."

She walked out the door and into the front yard. Tower followed her.

She stopped. Behind her was a divided sky. On one side, clouds the color of gunmetal stacked up and built a wall of possible rain. Lightning scratched white streaks against the thunderheads. On the left, the sky was clear and bright as a baby's eyes. A typical Florida horizon where it could rain on one side of the street and be sunny on the other side.

Tower gave it one last chance. "You want the truth, right? The one thing I know and remember from my days walking a beat is you have to have an open mind. Yes, I don't think Brady did anything. I could be wrong, but let the investigation prove it. What I'm saying is people still have to be careful, because if the killer is not Brady, then what?"

She didn't answer. T.O. took one long look at Tower before getting into her car and driving off. He was now consumed with the thought of why police had not contacted him about a clock countdown or a message. The only reason he could imagine was because there was no clock. And no reason to contact him. If so, he joined the police in theorizing why the carnage would stop now.

In the sky, the clear side was winning, pushing the darkness out of the horizon and reducing the threat of rain. The battle in the sky was probably not the only one Tower would witness that day.

He worked on the pile on his desk. Three more checks arrived for work done weeks earlier. Seventeen requests also arrived, asking for employee background checks, possible workman's comp violations, and seven letters saying Tower was already approved for a credit card. He turned on the CD player and listened to smooth jazz. Tower rejected the urge to sleep and turned off the music for a short trip to the ocean. There, he could think about Shannon and the investigation.

Something on the car demanded his attention. He kept his focus on the object on his windshield wiper.

A burner cell phone.

Tower didn't touch the phone at first. All his training as a police officer kept coming back to him. He examined the cheap phone, still deciding what to do with it, when it started to ring.

He was hesitant, his hands moving closer to the phone, hoping it would stop. The phone kept ringing.

"Hello." Tower looked around at his surroundings as he spoke.

"I hear you been looking for me."

"Stan? Stan Brady?"

"I hear you think I didn't kill anyone. And you would be right."

"Then why not go to the police?"

"Because they already think I did it. I need more time to figure this out."

The entire time Tower held Brady in conversation, he was listening for background sounds: a train noise, birds chirping, anything to give him an edge to determine where the call was being made. "You have a solid alibi for the days in question?"

"Days in question." Brady laughed. "You sound like a cop. That's cop-talk. I didn't do it."

"So, what did you do? What are you doing with Nat?"

"Leave him out of it."

"Where are you, Stan? I can come to you. Just give me a place. I'll be right there. We can go to Mark David. I'll take you there myself."

"Mark David, is that his name? The guy who keeps telling everyone I did this. We all know I didn't do this!"

"Then we'll tell them together. I'm not a lawyer but I can clear the path for you to give them your side."

Quiet.

Tower let him think. A certain clicking took up the sound void. Stilton Bay locations flashed through Tower's head in a quick race to match the sound with a place. Again, soft clicking or banging sounds. Metal on metal.

"I'll tell you what, I need to check on a few things and I'll get back to you."

Tower needed more time to listen. "You don't want to do that. If you get caught up in something, it will only be worse. Come to the police department with me now."

"I have two conditions. First, don't tell police about this conversation. I had to find your office location after someone tore up your card. Second, I'll contact you back."

"When?"

"Just hold on to that phone."

"Okay, Stan, but I have one condition. What are you doing with Nat?"

"He's my alibi. I guess I can tell you. I was a finder."

"You were looking for locations to break into?"

"Bingo. Ripped my jacket at one place. I didn't know her friend was killed until later. Told Nat hands off. But yeah, I found locations for them to rob." His voice jumped in volume. "I didn't take anything. They did all the taking. But Nat can vouch I was with him."

"Come in today. Right now. We can sort all this out."

The line went dead.

Tower waited for another call. The incoming number came up as unknown caller. He waited for several minutes and decided to move on. Tower kept thinking about the background noise. Much of Stilton Bay did not have that particular sound. He tried to match it but couldn't come up with anything. His guess was Brady was still in town. The other question before him was whether to pass on this contact with Brady to Mark David.

He went back into the house and heated up a cup of coffee. With the cup sitting on the table, wisps of steam lifting from the brew, Tower took his spoon and tapped the side of the cup. He kept tapping, trying to approximate what he heard on the phone. For sure, Brady was outside, because he heard a few birds. He tapped the cup again.

This time he slowed it down and tapped one more time.

He knew where the sound came from.

Tower grabbed the keys to the surveillance van.

35

Tower slow-rolled the van to a stop and looked out over the Stilton Bay Marina. Quiet and peaceful, with dozens of boats and a few yachts tied down in slips. The marina was very close to the forest park where police found the body of Kincade. All the yachts were motionless. Tower centered his attention on the sailboats and smaller vessels bobbing in the dark water. His first few scans of the marina showed no one moving about or walking the old planks of the place.

He did hear the occasional pinging of rigging on squeaky masts.

Tower knew he was in the right place, he just had to find some activity. He was looking for a liveaboard. Over the years, Tower had many friends who lived on their boat. Some even wrote blogs about making a boat their permanent residence. A few scant birds made the marina a soothing balm for a nervous soul. He could see why they chose this lifestyle. Once arrangements were made for water hookups, some attached a grill and the pungent aroma of burgers or shrimp drifted on the salt-sea air. Today, no one was grilling.

There was something bothering him. How did Brady know exactly when to call him if he was here in the marina? Somehow, someplace, the tall, lanky girlfriend must have helped by camping out in a car. In fact, Tower thought, she was probably the one who placed the phone on his car.

He could check in with the marina master and see if they knew of anyone living on a boat. Tower didn't want to bring any attention to himself, so instead, he just stayed low-key. He was prepared to remain in place for the night and look for any lights coming on in a boat.

His first mission was finding a place to angle his surveillance van so he could watch most of the marina. He parked in the shadow of a banyan tree. Next, he set up his tripod, sliding the legs into built-in slots. A camera mounted with a long lens came next. Tower promised himself if he saw or made contact with Brady, he would call Mark David. Until then, this was all wait-and-see.

Two hours passed. The rhythmic cadence of the soft pinging would easily put one to sleep. This was Tower's game.

Surveillance.

Tower had the patience of a sniper.

The soft sounds of the rigging were melodic, a way to caress the brain and become absorbed in the hypnotic calm. A woman walked by with her dog, out for a stroll. Three people pointed to the yachts, laughing as if they owned one. Surveillance was slow and tedious. There were long moments of thinking he might be in the wrong place, just wasting what valuable time he had. Tower gave in to the serenity and let his impulses slow down. He still kept his eye on the camera lens. Tower grabbed his second bottle of water and took a small sip.

Then she appeared.

The woman was wearing a hoodie pulled up over her head, tight jeans, and black sneakers. When she turned for just a flash, Tower recognized the face.

The spitter.

Tower watched Stan Brady's girlfriend stop and move the plastic bag full of food, shifting it to the other hand. She obviously had a long walk with the food and it was getting heavy. Food for Brady.

Her gait easily covered a lot of ground because of her long legs and stride. Tower started snapping photographs. He also picked up the cell phone.

Four rings and no Mark David. Voicemail.

Tower hated voicemail. He dialed again. Again, no answer. Besides voicemail, Tower hated to leave a message, especially this sensitive.

She stopped and looked around as if she could tell someone was watching her, yet she wasn't able to find the source of the eyes on her. The bag was eased down to the wooden planks. She was hesitant. Tower was convinced she could not see him. Her gaze whipped left and right without centering on a subject. She was looking.

Tower called again.

"Mark David…"

"Mark, get down to the marina right now. Brady's girlfriend is here dropping off food. It has to be for Brady."

"On my way."

Tower eased the phone down without taking his eyes off her. She just stood there. Tower remembered something. There was a small boat resting against the front of the house where she lived. But what was the name of the boat?

Tower whispered to himself, "What was the name." He didn't have time to check the photographs he had taken of the house, so everything was left up to his memory. The whisper became a soft roar. "What was the name, Tower?"

Little Mo.

The valued memory came to him. The tiny boat was called *Little Mo*. Somewhere in the marina, he reasoned, there had to be a *Big Mo*. She kept standing there as though not quite sure what to do. Tower did not want to lose track of her so he could not do a quick search of the boats floating in the marina.

She picked up the bag.

Maybe she was convinced no one was watching her. She was walking again, out of range from Tower's view. He had a decision to make: stay in the surveillance van or get out and follow.

Tower eased the van door closed.

The trick to a follow was blending into the surroundings while moving forward and not letting the target know you are in pursuit. Tower let her get ahead. She didn't have a lot of options. There were four slip extensions leading to dozens of boat slips. All he had to do was hide and wait. He watched her stop, then walk down the C concourse to the marina. Tower pulled out his cell phone and dialed Mark David.

"Go ahead, Frank."

"I've got her going into concourse C."

"Okay. My people will be there in a few minutes. We don't want to scare her off."

"Understood."

He put away the phone. Tower stood behind a gas station. For now, he was lucky no one was purchasing gas. Tower crouched down and looked at her through the narrow opening between the pumps. She was still looking over her shoulder. There, on her left, Tower saw his guess was correct. The *Big Mo*, a twenty-five-foot sailboat, was tied down. She took one last look around and then stepped onboard.

Tower stayed in place. He did not want to go down the concourse. Confrontation was not what he was planning. Several seconds later, everything changed.

She screamed.

The yell was so loud a couple far off turned around and looked for the source of the shriek. Tower could no longer wait for Mark David.

He ran toward the scream all the while looking for a suspect. The *Big Mo* was seven boats away on the left. The screaming did not stop. There was no sign of her, so she must have still been onboard. When he reached the sailboat, Tower took a very quick look for any police.

Nothing.

He jumped on the boat, careful to make sure no one was about to attack him. The screaming had stopped. He looked down into the hold. She was sitting there, squeezed up in a tight ball of legs and arms, holding on to herself. Tears rolled down her face. She seemed frozen in fear. Tower looked around and could not find anyone who might confront him. Then, on the table, he found what scared her.

Tower held out his hand. "C'mon. You are safe. Police will be here. C'mon, let me help you up."

He grabbed her ebony fingers and took both hands to guide her up to a standing position. Her crying was so intense, she was only able to breathe in short bursts, taking in just bits of air. One step, then a second step. She was like a baby, walking and sobbing, unable to get control of herself. A fast-food burger, fries, and several cans were all over the floor. The cans were still rolling to a stop in the pools of blood.

Tower helped her up to the deck and Detective Mark David. Jake May helped her off the boat, where Sania joined them. They took her away from the immediate area and walked back down the concourse. Tower was still down in the boat, looking up at Mark David.

"What do we have, Frank?"

"It's all yours, Mark. I'll get out of the way. When you're ready, I'll give you a statement."

Tower stepped up and was able to climb out of the hold without touching the railing. Mark David looked down.

There, on the table, resting on a dinner plate, was a human ear.

36

Tower knew his next couple of hours would be occupied by Mark David's questions. He sat and leaned against an oak tree, waiting to be interviewed. Tower also made sure he sat close enough to overhear what the spitter told detectives.

She told them her name was Leandra Crosland. She went on to explain, yes, she was delivering food to Brady and he was on the run for something he did not do. Four times, she insisted since he was not formally charged with anything, she was not harboring a fugitive. When they asked her about entering the boat, she pushed her hands up to her face and held them there. She said when she stepped onboard, everything was too quiet. He always met her right away and complained about the food and being cooped up. This time, she knew something was wrong. When she mentioned the ear, she choked up.

There was a moment when she got quiet. When David asked her who could be responsible for attacking Brady, she buttoned up. She did say it had to be Brady's ear because she recognized the diamond stud. Tower was convinced she had a good idea who cut Brady.

Tower was waiting to hear his name mentioned. Before she was asked about Frank Tower, there had to be a discussion about the murders. She denied Brady could possibly be involved. She was fuzzy about where he was on certain dates in question. Then, she was asked about Tower.

Yes, she was the one who put the burner phone on Tower's car windshield. Then, she waited to see him pick it up and signaled Brady to call. Several minutes later, it was Tower's turn to talk.

"Before you ask me anything, yes, I spoke to Brady." Tower stood up from his shaded spot.

Mark David flipped his notepad to a fresh page. "What did he tell you?"

"That he was running with the same three I mentioned to you before, Nat and the two others. And that he was scouting homes for them to break into, although he said he did not take part in the burglaries. He also said he was the one in the backyard at Janine Iwan's house, that he had no idea her friend was murdered."

"And about the murders?"

"He insists he had nothing to do with that."

Mark David was finishing up more notes. He looked up at Tower. "Okay, Frank, I know you're just busting at the seams to tell me how this all plays out."

"I believe him. I almost convinced him to let me take him to you. That close!" Tower pinched his fingers. "I figured out where he might be hiding. Heard the boats in the background when he spoke to me. After I set up and saw her, I called you right away. It would help if you picked up the phone when I call."

"And I'm supposed to be on call waiting for you. I'm busy, if you haven't noticed."

"Mark, I think Nat somehow heard Brady might talk to you and got to him. He probably doesn't have long before Nat takes it one more step."

"Without giving you any info, let me ask you this: what if the killer took Brady? If you are correct and Brady did not murder anyone, the real doer could be upset Brady's getting all the credit."

"Look at what happened? Someone took his ear. Was there a thumb drive left behind? Naw, I don't think our killer did this. I would look for Nat and I would hurry up about it."

Tower watched the crime techs leave. Mark David put Crosland in his unmarked and headed in the direction of the police station. More questions were in her future. Tower was hungry and exhausted. He really wanted to find food but put that idea off since he liked to keep the surveillance van hidden as much as possible. He drove home, got his bullet-in-the-door car, and drove to Ray's Restaurant for a snack. There, he could pore over the facts and pinpoint where to find Nat. Why wait for Mark David.

37

Ray walked to Tower's table and delivered the meal himself. He lowered the plate and set it before Tower. "I don't know, Frank, you order this more than anything else. We make it for you, but you're one of a kind."

"That's what my wife keeps telling me." Tower had his laptop and a notepad near him. For a moment, he wanted to enjoy his meal: a spaghetti sandwich. Three customers watched him take the first bite. The pasta was on two slices of toasted wheat bread. Tower ate and did not spill a morsel.

Halfway through his meal, he pulled the laptop in front of him. Tower knew there would not be much time for Stan Brady. A chopped-off ear meant a lot of blood. Even if they managed to control the bleeding, the pain would make him yell constantly. Nat wouldn't stand for that for very long. Brady would need clean bandages and something to stop any infection. The next few hours were critical if Brady was to stay alive. And the second set of circumstances, the Stilton Bay killer, as the newspaper now called him. Another victim could be snatched any moment. Tower reasoned if one bullet was fired his way, another was sure to follow, especially after a cut job on Brady. Blood emboldened a killer.

For Nat, any usual places for where he might be holed up didn't wash. Mark David probably checked them all by now. He had to be at a place where he could question Brady before finishing his life.

Tower wiped his mouth, paid the bill, packed up the laptop, and headed for his car. There was one place to check first.

Denton Drug Store was not attached to a chain. Not too far off the downtown district, Denton's was a short stop away from just about anywhere in the city. Known mainly to locals, Denton Drug was the place Tower bought his first pack of condoms. This was where teens got their acne cream. People on hard times could rack up an account and pay for things later. A chain drug store would never do that, and people remembered the gesture. The outside walls needed a fresh coat of paint, the tiny shopping carts never rolled correctly, and over the years the front windows were replaced twice after barely cognizant drivers crashed into the building.

Denton Drug had history.

Tower walked into the place. He picked up his pace when he approached the counter and followed close behind an employee walking inside a locked glass booth. A late-teen with short hair put up his hands as if to stop Tower.

"Where's Denton?" Tower eased the teen's hands back down to his sides.

"He's in the office. Who are you?"

"He's Frank Tower. I'll take it. C'mon in, Frank." Denton ushered Tower into his inner office and closed the door. Old man Milo Denton's body needed help getting around. He spent most of his time in the office watching all kinds of surveillance store cameras and checking the day's receipts. Denton didn't bother to get up, not since the knee operation failed to correct the problem. Eyesight poor, hands a little shaky, being eighty-three years old and still working was not pretty.

"Milo, got a minute?" Tower stared at the banks of camera monitors.

"For you, Frank, I got plenty of time."

"I'm looking for someone. You know a guy named Nat? Or maybe the two jerks he has working for him?"

Milo leaned back in the chair. Tower knew he was processing the question. "Nat, you say?"

"You know him?"

"Maybe."

"Trying to see if he was in here, buying say gauzes, cotton swabs?"

"Frank, you start'n trouble for me?" Milo's eyes bored in on Tower.

"Milo, normally I'd schmooze you a bit, but I'm in a hurry. Were any of them in here in the last hour or so?"

"Maybe."

"C'mon, Milo, it's time to tell me."

Milo pressed hard on the arms of his chair as he struggled to get up. When Tower started to help him, Milo knocked his hands away. "I can make it." Now erect, the two men were closer to eye to eye, only Tower was still a foot taller. "If that Nat fella finds out I spoke to you, he comes back in here and busts up my place."

Tower leaned in closer to him. "When was the last time you needed me?"

Milo started to sway a bit, then caught himself by hanging on to the chair. "I know. You helped me out at least four times. I owe you."

"I just need some direction, Milo. Then I'll take it from there. He won't know from me where I got my information."

"You sure?"

"Sure."

Milo grabbed a tissue and wiped his nose. "Yeah, that idiot, what's his name, the smaller kid that works with Nat, he was in here. Bought all kinds of medical wraps and booked it on out of here."

"And you know where they were going?" Tower backed up. "You know, Milo, 'cause you know just about everything that happens around here. Where would they be going?"

"Between us?"

"Between us."

"We made a couple of deliveries this summer. If you promise to keep it between us, then I'll tell you where I think they are right now."

38

Parkham Curve was the name given to a road once used as a shortcut to a plot of land where Florida vegetables were grown and sold. A pick-it-yourself vegetable place. One could pull over, buy a basket for a low price, search the bountiful yields, and pick tomatoes, cucumbers, and even strawberries. Now closed, the area was home to a few big houses. The original owners lived here and had enough room to build quarters for some hired help. The place Tower surveyed was now boarded up.

Tower parked his car far back up the road and came in through the large outgrowths of cocoplum and wild periwinkle. A neat and trimmed yard of mowed grass was now taken over by nature. Giant leafed philodendron hugged the live oak trees. Tower swatted away an airborne assault by mosquitos. His target was the rear window. The dark SUV was parked out front. As he got closer, he heard the moans.

Stan Brady was in pain.

The only problem was locating the source of the groans. On the lot were three moderately sized homes. If he broke into the wrong location, the end result might not be good for Tower or Brady. Tower's cell phone was showing a poor connection. He really needed to call Mark David. Again. Tower rang him and left the dreaded voicemail on the detective's phone. He also called 911, could not hear the operator, yet still gave information and left the phone on the ground so they could hear.

Until they came, this was all on Tower.

He stepped closer and stopped so he could listen. A voice permeated the air.

Kizner.

Tower was able to narrow down the source of the sounds to two buildings. Most of the windows were covered. He kept going, slow-walking until he reached the rear of one building. This was definitely the right spot. Tower inched up to the window.

Inside, he saw Stan Brady tied down with duct tape to a chair, facing away from him. A large wrapping covered most of his head. He needed to go to the hospital. Darvis Kizner, all one-hundred-sixty pounds of him, kept waving a knife at Brady. Tower listened while staying back and watching out for Nat and Duncan.

"We were about to cut you in for more." Kizner appeared to think about the phrase "cut you in" and started to laugh. "Cut you in." Tower couldn't understand all the words with him laughing so much. This was just about a moment when he would not be able to wait for Mark David. He touched the top of his Glock to reaffirm its place on his hip.

Kizner got serious. "We got too much going on here for you to start telling police 'bout stuff. Too much."

Duncan entered the room. "Nat said don't hurt him now. He wants to do the fixins."

Kizner moved back.

Tower texted Mark David with a *911!!!* Again, giving him the location.

Nat walked into the room. Brady labored to speak, pushing a towel up against the right side of his head. "No matter what I say, you're going to kill me."

Nat took the knife from Kizner. "How would you like to lose the other ear?"

Tower's thoughts pushed around several alternatives for what might happen in the next five minutes, most of them bad. Without the sound of sirens off in the distance, he had to act.

Now.

Duncan moved in on Brady, giving him a slap so hard he fell over with the chair, spilling the towel and giving a shrieking yelp. Duncan sat him up again.

Nat put the knife up close to Brady's face. "Last chance, Stan. What do the police know? How many people did you tell about this? You don't come clean and next we find your girlfriend."

"Didn't say anything."

"I don't believe you. Who knows?"

From outside, the four heard the SUV's alarm going off. Kizner ran to a front window. "The car's on fire." They left Brady. Out front the SUV was a blazing inferno. All three ran outside. Nat directed Kizner, "We got stash in the back seat. Get it out!"

Kizner looked like a man being asked to jump off a cliff. He pulled out the car keys, clicked on the fob, and opened the front door, only to see flames shoot out at him while eating up the fresh oxygen. "I ain't going in there."

Behind them, Tower was now inside the house and slammed the door shut. He locked the door. Outside, Duncan raised his gun and fired off two shots toward the house. Tower went to a window and momentarily placed his gun against the glass to show he had a weapon. Duncan, Kizner, and Nat took cover.

Frank Tower went back to the room where Brady was still next to the chair. There was glass everywhere from Tower smashing a window with his gun to gain entrance. He heard some commotion out front as he managed to get the tape off Brady. "Stay down. And stay away from the windows!"

Stan Brady found a middle spot between two windows and got on the floor. Tower returned to the front of the house and saw only Duncan and Nat outside. Kizner must have been trying to circle around to the back. Tower busted out the front window to show he was prepared to fire his weapon. Then he ran to the back of the house. Just as he entered the room, an arm reached inside the window frame.

Kizner.

Tower grabbed him and pulled Kizner inside. Kizner's gun dropped on the ground and Tower kicked it away. Before Kizner had a chance to figure out his situation, Tower came across his face with a hard jab, followed by two more quick punches. Kizner was down. Brady was up and kicking Kizner in the side. Two, three, four times. Tower had to stop him. Still no sounds of police.

Tower directed Brady to grab the duct tape and secure Kizner, then went back to the front. The moment Tower's face appeared at the window, two shots lasered past him. Best he could tell, Duncan was the shooter. Tower ducked. If he was going to use his Glock, this would be the moment. Tower was reluctant. He wasn't a cop anymore, and his actions now might be misconstrued in a courtroom, even if he thought he was the victim.

Three more shots.

This time Nat, using a small caliber weapon, fired off the rounds from behind a tree. The SUV was a smoldering black mess of metal and tires. Flames still licked the top.

Police cars roared up the road, kicking up a cloud of dust so thick it was hard to see how many were arriving. Duncan and Nat turned around, trying to stay hidden and out of Tower's gun range. Three uniforms got out, all of them yelling.

"Put your guns down! Now! Get on the ground!"

The officers did not back down. They kept coming. Big Jake May was next, followed by Mark David. Five guns were now trained on Duncan and Nat.

Nat dropped his weapon. Duncan did not.

He started firing. The officers yelled their commands one more time, giving Duncan one last chance to change his mind.

Two more shots from Duncan.

The first police bullet hit Duncan chest-center. Once he went down, the firing stopped. Duncan was not moving. Jake May kicked the weapon away from Duncan. Nat got on the ground and was handcuffed.

Mark David approached the front door. "Frank! You okay?"

Frank Tower opened the front door. He showed his hands to let them know he was not holding a gun. Once that was done, Tower pushed Kizner out the door. An officer moved up to the front of the house and handcuffed Kizner. Tower then helped Stan Brady outside.

Mark David called it in. "We've got one suspect down. Need a fire rescue at Parkham Curve. We have another, a male, with an ear injury. Please send a second rescue. Code three." Once David surveyed the area, there was another call. "Also please tell responding fire units an SUV is on fire and they will have to address that. Thank you."

Mark David pulled Jake May aside. "Make an assessment on what we have in the house, any other persons hurt. After you do that and the building is cleared, we'll wait on the search warrant and clean this up."

Jake May and two uniforms went through the house. Tower could hear them yelling "clear" as they moved from front to back. Jake reported back to Mark David. Fire units were now arriving. One unit put out the car fire. A paramedic checked Duncan for a pulse and asked for a gurney. It was not the paramedic's job to declare someone dead. Duncan was transported to the hospital and a doctor would carry out the final process of making a declaration on him.

Mark David looked at Kizner and Nat, each sitting in the back of a police car. Jake May was assigned to follow Stan Brady to the hospital, where he would be treated and questioned later. And booked.

May came over to Tower. "Frank, we're always cleaning up after you."

Tower showed him the butt end of his Glock. "Here's my gun if you need it. I didn't fire my weapon. And by the way, you're supposed to be the man smart enough to beat me here."

May left.

David took out his pad and spoke to Tower. "How did you figure out they were here?"

"Ah, I could tell you, but then I'd have to..."

"Funny doesn't cut it right now, Frank."

"I'm silent on that one for now. Promised someone. Just be glad you got here in time to save a life."

David aimed his pen at Tower. "We will have to take your gun. Won't be long. Routine."

"No problem." Tower looked at the house. "When you go inside, look at the room on the right."

"May told me. Looks like more than ninety thousand in cash, two cut-downs, four long rifles, a few knives, and ten bags of drugs."

"You forgot to mention one more thing."

David said, "I know. Looks like there are dozens of stolen driver's licenses from what Jake told me."

"Stolen identities. This was a lot bigger than just some home break-ins. These guys were running a nationwide identity theft ring."

"Thanks for your help, Frank."

"You'll be processing this stuff all night."

"I've got a killer to find, remember? The fraud division will take over. And the Florida Department of Law Enforcement will investigate our shooting of Duncan."

"Where are the owners of this house?"

Mark David put his pad away. "They're out of town, all summer as best we know. We called them. They are flying back. Some developer wants to turn this corner into twenty homes."

"For the record, I set the car on fire. Needed a distraction." Tower wiped a heavy line of sweat from the side of his face.

"So, you're convinced Brady is not the guy on the killings?"

"I'm convinced he's out there." Tower paused. "Still no hard drives?"

"With your name on it? No. We'll get a formal statement from you in a bit. Don't go anywhere."

"I don't mind going to the station."

39

Two hours after he gave a statement, Tower sat on a bench outside the Stilton Bay Police Department. His work would have to wait.

A weary Leandra Crosland walked through the front doors. She took one look at Tower and plopped her thin frame next to him. "They won't let me see him."

"What name do you go by? I'm guessing you don't use Leandra."

"Not since I was nine years old. I go by Andra sometimes. My nickname is Flower. Why won't they let me talk to him?"

"Not right now. He's still going through the booking process. After the doctors help him, next comes the police. First, they'll talk to him. If he helps with the investigation, and I really hope he does, that will determine what they do with him."

"Talk, huh?"

"Did the police ask you what you know about what these guys were up to?"

"Yeah, they did. I didn't know about any of this, I swear. I just know Stan did some side hustles."

"Those side hustles could get him five years in prison."

"He didn't do anything."

"If police think and can prove this is a big deal, and even if Stan had a small part, that's still a part that he has to answer for."

She sat back as if considering all kinds of options. "He might have to testify if he talks."

"Maybe. The key thing is right now he needs to tell them all he knows. Otherwise he could be caught up for things he had no knowledge of and that could get him even more years. Now, and I mean right now, is the time for him to talk."

She reached down and rubbed her right toe.

"You okay?"

"When I saw..." She paused. "When I saw that ear on the table, I knew it was Stan. The thing had his diamond stud in it. I tried to get out of there and I slipped on that first step. Damn near broke my face. Hurt my foot."

"You might want to find him a good lawyer. Make a deal with the state."

"He might not like that."

"That's where you come in. A bit of convincing on your part, and trust me, it's in his best interests."

She sat back on the bench, looking defeated. Both her hands rested on her lap and she gave up trying to smooth back her hair, letting a soft wind sort it all out. Andra's large brown eyes looked straight ahead, not really focusing on anything. "This has been a bad week. My place is a mess from police stomping around, my boyfriend is in jail, and someone cut off his ear. I have to get him out."

Tower could tell she was going through myriad emotions. A lawyer, a good lawyer, would cost a lot upfront. Did she have access to that kind of money? Maybe she could plead for Stan with a lawyer who would work for less. If Stan owned the boat, and sold it, that would be a good start. The problem was right now the boat was part of the evidence. Nothing could be done with it in the short-term. A bail bondsman could figure it out. When Tower did a computer check on Crosland, her line of profession was food-delivery services. She delivered breakfast for people too lazy to get it themselves.

She rose zombie-like and pulled off the hoodie. Tower saw her get into a faded older car with a missing wheel cover. He was about to get into his own car when a cell phone call came in.

"Frank?"

"Yeah, go ahead. Stu?"

"Something's happened. They just tried to kidnap Judge Smyth's law clerk."

"They?"

"Well, someone. It's a big mess. They got a scene near the courthouse."

40

The Stilton Bay courthouse was not large. Called a satellite courthouse, there were just six courtrooms. Two civil and four criminal. Tower parked near the municipal parking garage. There was an active search for a suspect. A uniform was hanging crime tape. Two other officers were blocking off traffic. Overhead was the noisy chuff of a police helicopter circling the sky. Tower could probably stay where he was, while the public was being channeled into certain areas. Police had blocked off streets and no one was allowed in or out.

Tower tapped his side for the reassurance of his Glock, then remembered he gave it to Mark David. He was there without a weapon. Officers moved throughout the parking garage. Tower reasoned this must be the exact location of the kidnap attempt. And more specific, Tower concentrated on the area designated for judges and courthouse employees, a part of the garage not open to the public. Access cards were needed. One evident flaw of the whole concept was someone could easily slip past the gate guard on foot and get into the secured part of the garage. Tower got out of his car and leaned up against the fender. He was okay there as long as he didn't try to go anywhere. All of the officers knew Frank Tower.

The swirling hum of the helicopter made officers yell to each other to be heard. Tower lowered his driver's side window and listened to the limited police talk on his store-bought radio scanner.

"Tall male, six-foot, wearing all black and some kind of mask." If this was their killer, the description would be the first anyone had heard. Three victims were never able to describe their attacker. Those crucial details died with them.

Tower heard officers setting up what they called a "box." A box included the roads to be blocked off. An officer had to really know the streets well enough to get on a radio in a heated moment and calmly ask which streets and roads needed to be closed down. Dispatch would assign police cars to close in the box. All the commotion made Tower think about his time in uniform. He missed the action. Dispatch comments peppered the air. "Suspect said to be holding something in his right hand. Maybe taser or a rag."

These were all very valuable pieces of information. Tower took out his binoculars and aimed the lenses toward the three floors of the parking garage. On the second floor, Tower saw a group of officers and Mark David. He couldn't see a victim. Tower looked left and saw paramedics talking to someone.

He found her.

The woman looked to be almost retirement age. She had glasses and the right shoulder of her business suit looked torn. Mark David walked over to her and she started waving her hands as she spoke. Then she made the motion of pinching her fingers.

She must have used pepper spray on the guy.

For the next few minutes, she played out what happened to her. Tower tried to read her lips but couldn't. The helicopter noise seemed to get even louder. Someone motioned as if asking her if she wanted to sit down. She shook her head. From all of her body motion, Tower reasoned she was feisty and someone picked the wrong person to grab.

The sniffers had arrived.

In police talk, sniffers were trained dogs. K-9. Tower saw three canine officers approaching Mark David. There was a small meeting and the dogs went off in separate directions. The appearance of the dogs made Tower put the binoculars away. If the target subject was nearby watching, Tower didn't want to be surprised by him. Tower positioned himself so everything was in front of him. His head was moving side to side like an owl, looking for any movement. Minutes later, one dog had moved to the ground floor and ventured out into the two walkways leading to the garage. Tower always respected their work. The dog moved with purpose.

Tower also knew he was inside a perimeter. And that meant he could not move. Unless he was having a medical emergency, Tower was locked in place. This was exactly where he wanted to be, at the epicenter of any action. A second dog was far off near a row of cars. He checked his watch. The search was now in its second hour. If the dogs came back empty and any room-to-room search was the same, Mark David might be tempted to open up the perimeter.

Maybe.

Three officers walked past him, all carrying their long rifles. Tower also noticed a police sniper on the roof of an office building. There wasn't much to do now except wait for an all-clear. Traffic would again move.

The female victim was no longer on the second floor of the garage. Mark David and his crew were gone. There were things to get done. If she got a straight-on view of her attacker, then a sketch could be done and released to the public. Tower was about to get into the driver's seat.

He saw a blur of something. Or someone.

The whole episode was a second, while looking left to right. Tower looked again. The person he saw was wearing some type of mask. The thing happened so fast, he couldn't even properly describe who or what was there.

Before he could focus on just what he saw, the image on the third floor of the next-door building was gone. Gone, gone, gone.

Tower started to move in the direction of the building, then stopped. A row of police cars and officers still blocked his exit. There was no one around to tell. He wouldn't dare call Mark David right now. Tower did the next best thing. He approached an officer on traffic lock-down duty.

"I think I saw someone in a window who might be connected to this case."

The officer looked up at the tall stack of windows. "I don't see anyone."

"He's gone now. If you get someone over there, or if you can get in touch with Mark David, maybe they can check out the third floor."

Tower saw the officer was deep in thought, mulling over the request. Tower had to just wait. Pushing the situation would not help. This was all up to the officer now.

"I'll make the call to Mark David. Please stay by your car, sir."

"No problem. Not moving." Tower retreated to the driver's side door. He sent Mark David a text.

Another twenty minutes passed before Tower and traffic were allowed to move. No matter what Mark David did now, Tower made it a priority. He was going to check the third floor.

41

There was organized chaos on the first floor of the office building. A single entry guard busy ushering people back into the building didn't have a chance to check on Tower. As he walked past the guard station, heading for the elevator, Tower noticed all of the surveillance screens were blank. Somehow, four monitors were showing white noise.

Tower entered the elevator, punched three, and stood toward the back. He wanted everyone in front of him. Four others stepped into the elevator, each of them complaining about standing in the sun waiting for re-entry into the building. All of them got off on two. Tower was alone with the elevator doors open.

The suspect could still be here.

Tower got out on the third floor and stood still. He wanted to listen for any movement or conversation. Off to his left, two offices showed business signs outside the door. Brokerage firms. What Tower wanted were the offices to the right. He tried to figure the exact location where the man would be standing. Tower stepped a few paces, ready for anything.

The office up ahead had a large vacant sign outside the double doors. He kept going. Tower walked as quietly as possible. Still, no other movement. Just him.

He reached for the door knob. And turned.

The pull on the door was slow and easy. Tower readied himself for a man in black. Once the door was open a foot or so, he stepped back. Before he went inside, he wanted to view what he could from the hallway. Most of the place was empty. A few desks were located in no particular order, all covered in a layer of dust. He waited for any sounds or movement.

Again, nothing.

Tower stepped inside. In quick movements, he looked left, then right, taking in information. In that scant one to two seconds, Tower saw another exit door on the left, along with a row of glass-enclosed offices. No one was in plain view. On the right was a large room meant for at least a dozen employees. Papers were on the floor. Tower took another three steps. Someone could still be hiding behind one of the desks. He took his time and checked each one.

Ten feet from him was a large office. This had to be the place where the man was standing. Tower was using all caution. He walked up to the door and stopped, leaning against it.

Now inside, Tower did a visual check. The room was empty. A printer was off to the right, next to a wall of empty bookshelves.

Up against the wall was a photograph.

Tower was set in place. The photograph was taped to the glass wall. Outside, Tower had a direct view of the parking garage. Everything was there, the few police cars watching traffic, the top floor of the garage and the exact location where Tower was once parked out on the street.

The photograph kept Tower frozen in his own self-imposed lockdown. He couldn't step forward, reach out, or do anything. The photograph held him there.

Tower moved up close to get a better look at the picture. He was shaken. More than anything, Tower wanted to examine the photo. He held back. Don't touch it, he thought.

He heard movement behind him.

Tower turned away from the floor-to-ceiling window and stared in the direction of the sound. The door started to swing open. No one entered. Tower prepared himself to fight. He looked around for anything he could use as a weapon. He saw a hand push the door wide open.

Two police officers entered the room, guns leading the way, gripped in the weaver-style. Tower waited until their eyes met his and he knew what he had to do next.

Tower raised his hands and arms in the air, stretched high toward the ceiling.

Mark David and Jake May walked past the officers. All four looked around before David gave the command to stand-down. His glare bored into Tower. "What are you doing here!?"

Tower still had his hands up. "I did tell an officer about something I saw and I checked it out."

"Before us?" Mark David motioned to Tower to lower his arms. "You touch anything?"

"Nothing."

The officers stood watching Tower. Both were young, Tower figured, in their late twenties. The taller one spoke. "There's no one on the floor."

"Thanks." Mark David waved them off. "You both can go." The officers left. David walked up to Tower. "Up to now, I've fought off two attempts to arrest you for obstruction of justice. I can't defend you anymore. You come bull-rushing into a potential crime scene, not once but twice or more."

Tower tried to stay patient. "Mark, take a look at the picture on the glass."

Mark David followed Tower's gaze.

Tower said, "How do you explain that?"

There on the glass wall was a photograph of Frank Tower standing on the ground outside the parking garage, holding his pair of binoculars.

42

Tower was dismissed to a spot outside the hallway while crime scene techs walked in and out of the office on the third floor. Tower was ordered to stay in one spot and was guarded by the two police officers he met earlier. They had orders to arrest Tower if he moved an inch. He stayed in one place, leaning against the wall.

All the loose time gave him a chance to go over what happened. Tower remembered the printer in the office had lights on. The machine had to have power. Someone could take a photograph on a cell phone and place the phone on the printer. More than anything, Tower had confirmation someone was watching him. He took out his phone and started making checks. The number on the door was 309. Tower looked up ownership of the building, yet that would not tell him ownership of an empty office space. Mark David was probably checking on the owner.

Mark David left the office. His next stop was Tower. "You're flying too close to the sun, Frank. You're about to burn up."

"If that means I'm getting close to the truth, then I'm not going to let up. You know me."

"Look, I can only hold these folks back so long. One more of these, and they're gonna arrest you. Too many times they show up and you're already there, stomping all over a crime scene. You're all in our reports. The time to stop is now."

"Just remember, this guy has targeted me. I'm not going to sit back for anyone and not look for him."

"But we need to lead, not you."

Tower digested everything coming from Mark David. His friend of more than ten years was right. No one wanted a P.I. doing a bigfoot all over potential clues to the case. Especially involving three murders and one kidnap attempt. If Tower was going to get any information on the judge's assistant, he had to back off. Now.

"Gotcha, Mark. I'll stay out of your way. In my defense, at every turn on this, I tried to reach you. It's not my goal to obstruct. I just want to get at this jerk before the clues dry up."

"We all want that, but you've got to understand we're doing all we can. The next time we encounter that bust-in-the-door-first attitude, we slap the cuffs. Understood?"

"Understood."

The two of them had been through just about everything during Tower's five years on the force. They once both showed up at a traffic stop and four minutes later delivered a baby in the back seat. The father was speeding to get to the hospital. Baby didn't want to wait. Seven times they stopped a burglary in progress, arresting a dozen people. When they shared information on a couple of cases, they both realized handbags being sold at an outdoor plaza were fake. The arrests made a mention on the national news. Twice they were given joint Officers of the Month awards. All the attention paved a path for Mark David to make detective. Tower eventually quit the force. He did not want to screw up an investigation. He had one question for Mark David.

"Can I go?"

"Yeah, get out of here."

Maybe a second question. "Did the judge's assistant describe her attacker?"

"Frank!"

"Okay, I'm going." When he reached the elevator, Tower pressed the down button with a piece of paper from his pocket rather than use his finger. Just before he got into the elevator, there was a yell from Mark David.

"Watch for a press release."

43

Tower retreated to his office. He checked the mail, replaced two AC filters, swept the front steps, and got on the treadmill set up in what was a back bedroom. Tower let jazz fill up the air and tried to push the events of a triple murder out of his head. For the moment.

Standing down was not something he liked to do. The Tower way meant connecting some serious dots and not letting anything stop you. The picture on the glass told him there was a chance he was being watched, just like the others. Someone wanted to see him squirm.

Seven minutes into the treadmill walk, he sped up the pace. He wanted to check on T.O., check on Janine Iwan, check in with attorney Stu, yet his mind told him to tap the brakes. Just slow down and let Mark David work the investigation. Without Tower.

Tower sped up the machine again. Now he was running. Maybe he would work the investigation out of his system. Twenty minutes in, Tower slowed back down to an easy walking pace. His gray sweatshirt was now dripping. He turned the machine off and walked out into his backyard. The area was small. Tower didn't mind. He only needed space for barbeques, a spot for the rare cigarette smoker. Tower didn't hide from the sun, sweat glistening off his forehead.

He stayed under the blast of the shower for almost twenty minutes.

Now dried off, Tower checked his phone. Six missed phone calls, four messages, and ten texts. His escape from the world didn't last long.

Tower had planned to stay off the phone, except for a possible call from Shannon. He wanted to stay low, just keep to himself and not call or text anyone back.

The knock at his door wasn't a knock. Loud banging. He checked the peephole. Opened the door.

Stu Baker stood there. "Been trying to reach you."

"You were on my list of call-backs. Been caught up."

Baker stepped into the realm of Tower's office, the converted home. "I went by your house. Nobody home. Then I came here." Baker was looking around the place before he found a chair in front of the big desk.

"When Shannon is out of town, I stay here. My mail comes here anyway."

"What happened with you and the police? I heard you went up into an office building?"

Tower weighed just how much he could share with Baker. "You'll have to check with homicide. I can't get into too much."

"Okay. I understand. You look like you're moving back away from all this."

"I just need to give everybody some space. I've been too involved."

Baker pressed his hands down on the chair as if he was about to get up. "Then maybe you won't be interested in what I have to say next."

Tower leaned on his desk, arms and elbows resting on the velvet mat. "Like what?"

"The judge's law clerk has been released from the police. We're trying to piece together all the facts. Trying to understand this."

"We?"

Baker eased back down in the chair. "Let's just say we think you know more about this case than anyone. And that there's a lot you're not saying. What if you met with the clerk and compared information?"

"Man, you are really trying to get me in trouble." Tower rubbed his chin. "I'm toxic."

"Tox?"

"Toxic. You don't want to come anywhere near me. I have to stand down."

"That doesn't even sound like you. C'mon, Frank. If this guy targeted her, she can't have police protection twenty-four-seven. There's some thought to maybe hiring you to watch over her. Is that possible?"

"I've got to think about it."

Baker checked his watch. "You've got till a bit later. Call me. Let me know what you want to do." He got up.

Baker walked out, closing the door with a soft push. Tower reached down and opened his safe located under the desk. Once open, he pulled out his backup Glock.

He was armed again.

He considered a next move. He strapped up the Glock, grabbed the car keys, and headed to the beach. Time to think.

Stilton Bay beach was a calm comfort. Incoming waves and salt-scented air always soothed him. The beach scene reminded him of the first time he saw Shannon. A strong wind had blown the hat off her head and the thing was rolling away from her. Tower ran over, picked it up, and saved the straw hat before it hit the water. He gave it back to her. A meeting on the beach that resulted in a marriage.

Tower let the air wrap him in caressing breezes. He sat on the warm sand and just let thoughts move in and out.

Then Tower stood up.

He pulled out his phone and called Stu Baker. "Stu, is that meet-up still possible?"

"Yeah."

"Good. Is there any way the judge can join us?"

"You know he really shouldn't get involved. I don't think that's a good idea."

"But I think he is involved."

"What?"

"Stu, I just figured out the killer's motive."

44

Stu Baker stood outside Tower's office seeking shade. When Tower walked out, he went right for the hard question. "What is it?"

"I can't say at the moment. I need your help with something." A look of desperation was burned into Tower's face. "We don't have a lot of time. The judge's clerk was attacked at the courthouse. This guy is getting too bold. I want to set up a meeting but I can't do it without your help."

"Careful. Didn't you say you were backing down so the obstruction charge won't come flying at you?"

"I know. This is too important."

"A meeting. What are you looking for?"

Tower almost sounded like he was pleading. "Like I said on the phone, any way the judge can be convinced to meet with us?"

"Legally speaking, that's a tough one. Now you want to pull a judge into your obstruction case. If I were the judge, I wouldn't come near you."

"I want to bring some people together who can help me flush this out. I can't do it unless I get everyone there."

"And you want me to approach the judge." Stu Baker was shaking his head.

"I know I am asking for a lot. But I have to pull this group together."

"Without the police..."

"Yep. Without Mark David, that's correct. He's too busy and I could be really wrong in my thinking. I just need everyone in one room. Once I get that, I know whether or not I'm close." Tower spoke louder. "We have to move faster right now to catch this guy. He's not going to stop. Throw out the rules and legal ethics and help me put this together."

Tower called it the tipping point. The moment in the conversation when another person had heard enough information and was in the wheel-churning process of agreeing or not. He could see it in Baker's face, a look of weighing several factors and coming to a conclusion. A decision. The tipping point.

Baker gave a half-smile. "We're crossing a lot of lines here, Frank. A P.I. setting up a meeting with a judge. Discussing a possible murder case."

"You and I know the judge will never be appointed if there is an arrest. He's too connected because of his clerk. He can talk about it."

"Well, no, he can't. I shouldn't even be getting into this."

"Stu, decision time."

"Okay. I'll contact the judge."

The tipping point.

Frank pointed to his house-office. "We can meet here. Whenever the judge has time."

"And if he says no?"

"Plan B and C. Sell it, Stu."

"I'll call you later. Man, this better work."

Tower said, "You help me get everybody together and we'll find out."

Three hours later, Stu Baker called Tower. "I got him. He's coming. He's extremely reluctant. Says the police should handle all this and we should stay out of the way."

"And you said?"

"I said what would his clerk want us to do? Then he agreed to come."

"Great."

Stu cleared his throat. "But, and there's a big but. The judge could change his mind at any moment. So when he gets there, the rest of the convincing is up to you."

45

By the time Stu Baker arrived at Tower's office, several chairs were encircling the desk.

"Where do you want me to sit?" Baker sized up the chair arrangement.

"Give the judge the big chair. Otherwise, sit where you want."

The knock on the door was slight. Tower opened it to see a woman about five-foot-five with round glasses, hair cut at the shoulders, and a black purse. She wore a gray business suit and a white blouse. "Are you Mr. Tower?"

"I am. Come on in. The judge is going to sit over there." Tower looked out the window. He had parked his own car a half-block away to leave space for the cars he was expecting.

"Hello, Mr. Baker." She didn't smile. When she reached her seat, she flashed a look at Tower. "I forgot. My name is Anna Strand. You know, like the Strand in England."

"Thank you for coming. Sorry to hear about your encounter. Are you okay?"

"My wrist is sore. I used up two cans of pepper spray on him before he took off."

Tower smiled. She remained serious. "The others will be coming soon."

Baker questioned, "The others?"

The knock was solid. Tower recognized the sound and the person. T.O. walked into the room and looked around with a quizzical expression. "Wow, I didn't know this was going to be a party."

"Just two more people and we can start." Tower showed his group a cooler filled with crushed ice and bottles of water. The knock was clear. When Tower opened the door, Janine Iwan was standing next to Judge Wayne Onid. Both of them looked surprised at seeing each other away from the courthouse.

Tower showed him the chair. "Judge Onid, please take the chair."

"Wouldn't hear of it! Let Janine sit there. I can sit in the back." He was the same height as Tower only eighty pounds heavier. His voice rumbled and would command respect, even if he had a job other than a judge. He wore a suit just the perfect shade of politician blue.

The judge stopped, then turned around. Tower was now facing the judge's back. Tower spoke low, his words chock-full of decorum. "Your Honor, I know you don't want to be here. We're probably breaking a lot of your personal rules. We're here for the victims."

The judge turned back around. "You know what could happen if the police find out we're here talking about this case?"

"There is no case before you, Your Honor. No case at all. Just the fact that someone attacked your clerk. The police are doing everything they can to find a killer, but I'm just asking you to listen to what I have to say. That's all, just listen. My effort here is to give something to the police they can use. I'm not going to do that until I tell it to this group first."

The tipping point.

Judge Onid blinked a few times and stared at his clerk. "Okay, I'll stay. I hope I don't regret it."

"Thanks, Judge. C'mon in." He sat down.

Tower stood in the middle of the group. "I want to thank everyone for coming. If anyone feels uncomfortable about being here, please, you can go at any time. No one is going to question you. We are just here to explore some facts."

"And a theory, I presume." Judge Onid sat off to one side.

"I have to admit, right now, it's just my side of things. Let me tell you up front, the police warned me not to do any more. What we're doing here now, I think, does not go against that warning. We are just talking. Just talk. I am glad Anna is okay. She was able to fend off an attacker. For others here, you have suffered a great loss." Tower went to another room and came back, rolling a white board into the room. On the board were the victims' names.

Tower took a deep breath. "We mourn for the victims. But I think their deaths were all aimed at getting back at you. Everyone individually in this room."

A round of disagreement filled the air. Tower let it all simmer. Baker spoke first. "You're saying Kincade's death was a way of making me suffer?"

"Yes." Tower pointed to the board. "Each one of you suffered the loss of your best friend. That was the killer's real intention. To kill the friends of the people he hated the most."

Janine Iwan raised her hand like she was in a classroom. "I can't believe you're pushing this on us. There is simply no truth to any of this."

"No?" Tower tapped on the board, going from one name to the next. "These victims have nothing in common. Not one single thing. Nothing. However, take a look at the people in this room. The friends of the victims. All of you have a lot in common."

"The courtroom." Judge Onid was somber.

Tower tossed a question. "Was there ever a time all of you were in the courtroom together?"

Baker scratched his head. "I can't remember anything like that. Judge Onid does civil court. He's done that for years. There is no connection."

"There is." Anna Strand pulled her purse closer to her body. "Judge wasn't always in the civil division. For years, he was a criminal court judge."

"I remember." Baker's eyes lit up. "At first I didn't remember, but now I do. I was in front of the judge."

Tower looked at Janine. "And what about you?"

"Well, yes. I was called upon as a witness for the state many times to talk about living conditions of a home, health care, and the well-being of a child."

Everyone in the room stared at T.O. "Why are you all looking at me? I don't remember anything. I just know my friend Preston is dead. I haven't heard one thing to tell me who did it and why."

Tower pressed her. "T.O., you're the key in this. There has to be one case. One criminal case that links everyone in this room. And it begins with you."

T.O. got up. Her hands were swinging at nothing. "I'm not the key! I don't know what you're talking about. I am not the main one in this. I'm not! I'm not!" She ran to the door, turned the knob, and sprinted into the street. The door was left open. Tower turned to the group. "Anna, how long have you known the judge?"

"Since we were in high school."

"Friends then?"

"Yes. Almost date friends, but he met someone else."

"And now?"

"Yes, I would have to say outside of his late wife, we're pretty good friends."

Judge Onid looked at Anna, then the group. "I agree with you, Tower. If something happened to her, I'd be a physical and mental wreck the rest of my life. So this is what this is all about?"

Tower again tapped the board. "I'm going to find out. Anna, can you do a bit of research? Find out if T.O. comes up in your database. Maybe her family or family member was in court. Maybe her father was in court. See if you can find her in the system. Would that be okay?" He looked at Iwan. "Janine, check your records. See if T.O. comes up as a child in need of your help. There has to be a case."

Anna looked at the judge as if she needed his okay to check the files. He nodded. "Yes," she said. "I can work on that."

Tower walked to the door. "I am convinced someone is watching you all suffer the loss of your friend. Taking joy in seeing you agonize. Please watch your back."

"The memorial service." Iwan stood up. "Somebody put a camera out there to watch us in mourning."

Baker walked out and kept the door open for the others. "Thanks for everything, Frank."

"Again, thanks for coming. I will follow up with T.O. And when I have all my facts right, I'll contact Detective Mark David."

46

The house-office emptied out and Tower was left with a stack of directives and leads to follow. He was about to get on the computer when there was a knock at the door.

"Hello, T.O."

She immediately walked over and plopped down on the couch. "It's all my fault."

Tower pulled up a chair next to her. "What has happened is not your fault."

Her eyes were focused on the floor. The muscles in her arms taut, eyebrows converged into an angry V. "I think about Preston all the time. And now, maybe I helped get him killed."

"This is exactly what the killer wants. He wants you to feel at fault. What you, what we all need to do, is concentrate on who has the motive. This is somebody in your past. Not just you but Stu the attorney, Janine the social worker, and the judge. One case. But I want to be clear about something." Tower gave himself a few seconds to get the wording right. "In finding this guy, it's all on us, not you. If you're not up to delving into your past, that's fine with me. That's why I told people the door was open. I don't want to put any pressure on you. We can work this out without you. No pressure, you got that?"

She let the words sink in. "No, I want to help. Do whatever I can to find him." T.O. looked straight into Tower's eyes. "Let me help."

"Okay." Tower moved back in front of his laptop. She joined him at the desk, taking a chair. "I tried tracing you back. I know what house you lived in, I know your parents. I have all that information. But there's a long period where I don't have any information."

"I'm trying hard, but I can't remember right now. There was a time I was away from my parents, staying with my aunt here in Stilton Bay. Something happened." She shook her head. "It wasn't my aunt. It was a friend of the family. A friend, I'm sure about that. I don't know why, but I was with her till I was about twelve. When I moved back with my parents, that's when I met Preston."

"Okay. You remember what street you lived on? An address? Or name of this friend?"

She got up from the chair, walked to the wall, and pretended to punch it, stopping before her fist met the wallboard. "I've tried and tried. I can't remember anything. A name, a street, nothing."

"Forget about names. Think about foods you ate then. What fragrance did she wear? What about shoes? You remember a store where you went shopping?"

"Let me think." She came back from the wall and sat on the arm of the couch. "I remember cherries. She always smelled like cherries."

"Okay, that's a start." Tower was typing. "Do you ever remember going to court for any reason? Maybe testifying."

"No. Now something like that I would remember."

Tower's next question was soft in tone, yet strong in what it could mean. "Did anyone hurt you?"

"I thought about that several times. There is a cloud that is trying to part. Something did happen. And then it gets all blurry. When I'm not thinking about Preston, I think about that cloudy part of my life and if something did happen to me."

"I did a court system check and I don't see your name anywhere. I'll check later with Anna. If you were a victim, that information, like your name, could be sealed by a judge."

"I'm trying to think if I talked to a detective."

Tower wrote a line in his notebook. "Good point. I can follow up on that." He put the pen down. "Don't beat yourself up. We're all trying to remember. Just relax and we'll see if things come back to you. During my time on the force, I don't remember meeting you." Tower went back to writing notes. T.O. moved to the soft couch pillows and leaned back. Tower let her think about her past. He didn't want to make a big deal, lest he cause her to freak out. Still, he knew anything she might recall could break the case open. And, Tower reasoned, that simple fact might put her in danger. Rather than send her out the door, maybe he should keep a closer eye on her. She closed her eyes and slept.

Tower's cell phone rang. He caught it on the second ring in hopes of not waking up T.O. "Tower."

"It's Anna."

"Anything?"

"I was able to use a tracking system I have. Using your name, the judge, Stu Baker, and Janine, I came up with one-hundred-seventeen cases. Now, when I look at your name, some of those cases have to do with a..." She sounded like she was going down a list. "Have to do with a woman named Jackie Tower. Is that your mother?"

"That's just Jackie. Not my mother." He paused. "She is my biological. You know what I mean."

"I think I get it. Well, this gives us a start. Unfortunately, that's a lot of defendants. And I cannot find, what's her name? I know she goes by T.O., but using her real name, I can't find one single case associated with her."

"You search her name by itself?"

"Yep. Looked and searched and double-checked. Nothing. Can she help you on your end?"

"Not yet. We're working on it."

"Okay. Gotta go. Long docket this afternoon. Stay in touch."

"Will do." Tower put his phone on the desk. He kept thinking to himself, one-hundred-seventeen cases. Somewhere in that stack was a killer. He was determined to find him.

His phone rang again. "Tower..."

"So formal."

"Hey, Shannon. Almost packed?"

"Packed and coming home tomorrow. Can't wait to see you."

"You need me to pick you up at the airport?"

"Naw, I know you're busy with cases. I'll be fine."

"You sure?"

"I'll call you once I get to the house. I'm sure I'll need to air out the place."

"The AC is on. I just stay here at the office when you're away."

"Get some sleep, remember to eat. But I know you won't do that."

"I promise. I promise. Have a nice flight."

"Sleep tight. Bye."

Tower put the phone down again and heard the soft hum of T.O. in deep sleep.

47

Tower waited in the lobby of the police department. The time spent sitting on hard plastic reminded him of a situation. One morning, just after he joined the Stilton Bay force, he was sitting at the desk, behind the heavy bullet-resistant window cage. A woman came in all frantic and yelling about a naked man outside who was refusing to leave. Tower couldn't get the attention of another officer, so he had to leave his post at the phone desk and check it out.

Outside, the man indeed was standing there naked. When Tower inquired, the man was ready to be arrested. Tower asked him when was the last time he had a meal? Almost two days ago, he replied. Tower figured it out. The man was so hungry that in order to get a meal or two, he came to the police department, stood by the front door naked, and waited to be arrested. An arrest would assure him of a place to sleep and more importantly, a meal.

Rather than arrest him, Tower made arrangements for the man to get some clothes from a lost-and-found bin at the department and asked a couple of police volunteers to take him to get something to eat. They even got him some food vouchers for a few more meals.

Tower sat in the lobby. No naked man in need out front. Just Tower sitting on hard plastic, waiting for Mark David. Tower followed him into the homicide unit. For the next twenty minutes, Tower unveiled his theory of connecting the dots to the friends of those murdered. He left out details of the meeting with the judge.

"Interesting." Mark David wasn't writing anything down.

Tower said, "So, you don't believe me. Rather, you don't think the facts fit. Mark, you know details that I don't. There's a lot that's not public. But I think this guy has been planning this for a long time."

"I'll have to get back to you."

"I know this is a one-sided conversation. You can't discuss stuff with me. But he's getting revenge for this one case. And since he's targeting me, it must have been one of my arrests. I just can't pin it down yet. Maybe you can."

"This room is empty because everyone is out there following up on leads. We're not resting. Your version will be thrown in the mix. I promise. And we're making some sort of announcement later. A short press briefing."

Four minutes later, Tower was back in his car headed to the office. He waited for a phone call from T.O. that didn't come. Tower was hoping she might remember a morsel of information. Anything to point him to an investigation. He turned on the television just in time to hear a reporter. She was doing a live report from in front of the police station.

"Just a few minutes ago, a police spokesperson announced another dire warning for the public. The police are asking people not to travel alone for now, that with the recent murders anyone is vulnerable. They are asking people to carpool, travel in pairs or groups. Just be careful."

Tower turned off the television.

The front door opened.

Once she was in the door, Janine Iwan was talking and moving. "Sorry, the door was open. I can't rest." She put her laptop on Tower's desk. "I keep going over all my cases back then and I cannot find any single incident or contact involving, what's her name?"

"T.O. is her nickname. Laura Corpin."

"Corpin. Well, I make out my initial contact reports. Not all of that information goes to a court file if no charges are filed. What I'm thinking is maybe this was a case that never made it to court?"

"That doesn't fit. The killer has picked out the four of you for a reason. We have to figure it out."

She brushed back her gray-black hair. "Well, you're stuck with me. My friend is dead. I hate to think it was because of something I did."

"Please remember, you were doing your job. Whoever this is was probably guilty of something."

Janine walked around the room. "I'm going home. You call me if you think there's something I need to check out."

"No problem."

She packed up the laptop and left. For the remainder of the night, Tower used whatever tricks he could to track down a vital clue. He went to sleep but found any attempt to close his eyes useless. The warning for the public, the three murders, a kidnapping attempt, all of it kept him awake.

In the morning Tower showered. The warm water felt good. He cooked eggs and one slice of toast. He mapped out what he could do throughout the day. Just after ten a.m., he got the call.

"Frank, it's Mark. Get down here right away."

"What is it?"

"We got another thumb drive. Just get down here, now!"

48

When Tower pulled into the police station parking lot, Mark David was waiting for him. Tower got out of the car and ran with him to the entry doors.

"What is it, Mark?"

"We'll start when we get inside."

Tower walked into the homicide unit's conference room. A large viewing monitor was set up. The entire team was there. As Tower entered the room, a few looked down at the floor, avoiding any eye contact with him.

Tower sat down.

Mark David rested his hand on a laptop. "I'm going to play this, Frank. I want you to know we're all here working on this together." He opened a file. Tower was very familiar with the look of the file. It had to be from the killer.

On the screen was a message:

FRANK TOWER YOU CAN'T SAVE THEM ALL

RAY – SHANNON – JACKIE

DO I HAVE ALL THREE? MAYBE

AT ZERO ONE WILL DIE

The countdown clock was moving. Mark David pulled the laptop back a few inches and positioned himself so he was in Tower's face. "This came to us by courier. The countdown clock gives us four hours."

Tower mumbled a response. "Four hours?"

"The team is working on this. Ray has to be Ray the restaurant owner. We tried but we can't contact him. His restaurant is closed. Jake called the Never Too Late and they said she ran an errand. We can't reach her. I've got patrols at both locations going through the area."

Tower repeated himself. "Four hours..."

"Frank, where is Shannon right now?"

Tower checked his watch. "She was due to arrive by plane. It should have landed two hours ago."

"You heard from her?"

"No, not yet." Tower rubbed a hand over his face. He had to come to grips with the situation. He pulled out his cell phone and called Shannon. Ten seconds later he got Shannon's voicemail. "Yeah, this is you know who. I must be busy. Leave a message and I will get back to you."

Tower's energy moved from shock to action. "You can tri-angulate their phones."

Mark David stayed calm. "We're on it. We tried that. Shannon's phone must be off. The staff at the Never Too Late say Jackie almost never takes her phone with her. We did a welfare check and found Ray left his phone on the desk in his office."

Tower stood up. "So, all three are missing and presumed kidnapped?"

"We don't know that. The message didn't say he grabbed all three."

"But he made it clear one will be dead." Tower used his cell phone to set up the countdown feature to match the exact time left on the thumb drive.

03:58:27

He had about four hours to locate all three. For a brief moment, Tower thought about the tortured souls found at locations around Stilton Bay. Ray was a friend like the others who were killed. Shannon and Jackie were family. He tried not to think of them in the same situation as Preston Wakefield.

Tower addressed the room. "What do you want me to do. I'll do anything." He now understood why no one would look directly at him. A powerless feeling moved into Tower like a festering sore. Giving in to the gloom was not Tower's way. He also understood why no one answered his question. Tower answered it himself. "Mark, just keep me informed. I trust you."

Tower turned to leave the room. Mark David put a hand on his arm. "Just keep us informed." Tower almost ran the hallway to the exit. He smashed open the front doors so loudly the officer in the glass cage stood up. Tower got in his car and drove toward his home. Not the office. Home.

When he got there, a Stilton Bay police car and officer were out front. Tower went inside. Stale air embraced him as he entered the living room. No one had cooked here in days. He went room to room. No sign of Shannon. He checked the landline phone. While most of the country went to cellphone-only living, Tower still believed in keeping a phone in the house. No messages. He left the house, waving a thank you to the officer.

Next stop, the Never Too Late.

While he was driving, he called Shannon seven times. Voicemail each time. Tower powered under the I-95 expressway going twenty miles over the speed limit. His stop in the parking lot was a screeching slide of burned tires. Four people were outside the entrance standing around talking. As he approached them, all the conversations were on Jackie.

Tower went inside. The woman at the desk looked frantic. Tower tried to keep his voice level. "Still no word from Jackie?"

"No."

"Did she say where she was going?"

"Just that she had a couple of errands. I didn't think it was anything. She had some brochures to pick up but I think she got them yesterday."

"You see anything or anybody?"

"No, it's been quiet." A large tear rolled down her cheek and plopped on the desk. Before Tower could say any words of comfort, she used both hands to wipe away the drenching of more tears to come. "I just want her found." Her lips were shaking.

"So do I." Tower handed her his business card. "If you hear anything, or she contacts you, please give me a call."

She took the card.

Tower was back in the car. Thirty-five minutes had passed. Thirty-five precious minutes. He had to make better use of the time he had left. He checked his clock.

03:43:23

Twenty-two seconds. Twenty-one seconds. Twenty.

He smashed the gas pedal.

T.O. met Tower outside her apartment complex. She ran to his car and moved inside. "I got your text. Your wife is missing?"

"Maybe. We're looking for her along with two others. Are you up for a short trip?"

"Sure."

They stopped seven minutes later in a working-class neighborhood, where usually both parents had a job to secure all the bills. Tower got out and watched T.O. "You remember this, T.O.? This is where you met Preston."

She got out and walked around a bit, inspecting the homes and landscaping. "It was a long time ago."

"Not that long. You're in your early twenties. Did something happen here, T.O.?"

She kept walking around. With a burst of excitement, she pointed to a house. "I used to live right there. And Preston lived two doors down." Her smile faded to a frown. "I'm trying but I keep thinking I have repressed memories about something."

"Take your time. Keep walking and looking. Maybe something will come to you." Tower took a quick glance at his phone. No messages. Nothing from Shannon or Mark David. T.O. stopped. "Everything here growing up with Preston was good. The bad stuff didn't happen here."

Tower rushed to his car, pulled out the laptop, and placed it on the hood. He waved her over to him. "If you lived somewhere else, I don't have a record of it. Maybe it was an apartment? Or boarding house? We have a few here in the city."

T.O. stared off toward a row of oak trees. He could see she was deep in thought. He stepped back and gave her space. Then, he posed questions in as soft a voice as possible. "Think of your living space. Was it just you? Maybe you had a friend before Preston?"

"That's it. I did have a friend. What was her name?" T.O. rubbed her fingers into her head. "Think, T.O.!" Her long stare at the trees continued. "Trouble, trouble, trouble. I was in trouble. I was in trouble. Trouble. Trouble."

Tower left her alone.

This was her world now. He got her this far. Now, it was up to her to research muddled memories and bring back a clue. What she did next shocked Tower.

T.O. slapped herself.

Then, she slapped again. And again. Tower stopped her from another rip at her own face. "What is it, T.O.? What do you remember?"

"He slapped me. Hard. Told me if I ever told anyone he would keep slapping until my skin tore off. I must have been twelve years old."

"Why did he slap you?"

"'Cause I was protecting my friend."

"What friend? Who was it?"

"Think, T.O. Think." Her eyes were shut.

Tower put his arm around her. "You are safe now, T.O. It's okay to tell me. Just let it out. Who were you protecting? Who was it?"

"Reena. Reena May Solum. My friend. Her mother was being beaten up and we tried to stop it. It was bad, Frank. We tried to stop it."

"What happened? I'm here, T.O."

"He would get drunk. Her mother would get mad 'cause of all the drinks. One night she knocked them over."

"Them?"

"Beer cans."

"Cans?"

"Yeah. He liked to put beer cans on the coffee table. She hated that 'cause they left all those little circles on the wood table."

"Then what happened?"

"One night she got angry and knocked over some like bowling pins. He hit her. Kept hitting her. Me and Reena did what we could. No one would do anything. Nothing. I couldn't just let her get hit anymore."

"So you did something?"

"I went to the telephone and dialed 911. I didn't say anything. I just dialed. He slammed the phone down. But it was too late. He slapped me. I ran out of there."

"You go home?"

"I ran outside and I waited. I was so scared. The police came." T.O. stared into Tower's face. "I saw a picture of you on the wall in the office. I remember more. It was you, Frank."

"Me? What picture?"

"The picture of you in uniform. When the police arrived, it was you. You were there. Then I ran home. After I found out Reena was okay and her father went to prison, I never wanted to go back there. Ever. I tried and tried to forget about it. Just forget it!"

Tower was done with questions. He was enveloped in thought. He played the time and place in his mind on just when the arrest was made.

T.O. looked like she was in a trance. The words came out as if she were in hypnosis. Tower had some vital information. Now, he needed to get in touch with Janine Iwan and Anna with the judge's office. He had to bring T.O. out of it and make her realize she was in a good place now. "I'm sorry."

"There's no need to be sorry."

"I put this all away in my mind. Never to come back. How is this connected to Preston?"

"We are very close to finding out." Tower picked up the phone to call Janine.

T.O. just kept repeating, "Reena was my friend. She was my friend."

49

Tower drove through two red lights, resulting in a long stream of honking horns and a raised middle finger. His mission would not wait for red, yellow, or green. He pulled up at Janine Iwan's house. She was waiting for him. Tower guided a sullen T.O. out of the car. "Watch over her." Tower could not stop moving. He let T.O. walk baby steps to Janine. "Thanks for doing this."

Janine Iwan grabbed T.O.'s hand. "She'll be fine."

Tower moved toward his car, his eyes still locked on T.O. "She says after the arrest, she never told anyone. Her parents, no one. It's stayed her secret until now."

"I already entered the name you gave me into the computer. I remember Reena. I'm going to text you all the information I can. I'm doing this for Saneele. Where are you going?"

"I've got to hunt this guy down. Did he really do time? And where can I find him?" For now, Tower was headed to his office. He changed his mind and pulled over, tires spitting rocks as he screeched to a stop. Tower opened the laptop and called Janine again. "You find anything?"

"You don't give me much time, but yes, I found something. I was out to that house seven times because Reena was skipping class and the school district was about to hold her parents responsible. The house visits were a mess. During that entire time, I never saw T.O."

"What was the father's name?"

"Randall Solum. I am sending you information on his date of birth. You can find out what happened to him. I don't have that info."

"Thanks. One more thing. Please pass all of this information on to Mark David."

"I will."

Tower put the phone down. Once he got the information from Janine, he entered the name and DOB into his search sites on the computer. Tower took out a pad. His next move depended on what he found.

He started drawing up a profile. Randall Solum, no middle name, was now fifty-four. He had just one child, Reena. His wife, Candice Solum, was forty-nine. From what Tower could determine, Candice and Reena moved to the Tampa area. Randall was accused of the attempted murder of his wife. Tower looked up reports detailing her injuries of two broken ribs, a punctured lung from a stab wound, a fractured cheek, arm bruises, leg bruises, and reduced hearing in one ear from a kick. Tower felt his temper going into the red zone, and he had to control it or he would lose focus on what he needed to do.

Randall Solum was sent to the Benson Institution to serve fifteen years for beating his wife. Tower's phone rang.

He knew the voice. "Hello, Mark. Did Janine call you?"

"Yes, but you've got to let me take it from here. Are you hearing me, Frank?"

"Just tell me, is this Randall Solum still in prison?"

"If I answer you, are you going to let my unit handle this?"

There was a silence. Tower didn't want to commit to anything. "Mark, if it was your loved ones and you had the power to do something, would you just do nothing?"

"Leave it to my unit. That's all I'm saying. Solum was released from the Benson Institution just over a year ago."

"So, he only did nine years. Got out early. And where is he now?"

"No information on that. Upon his release, there was no probation. He doesn't even have to report to a parole officer. He was free to go."

"And a picture?"

"You promise to let my guys do their thing. Thanks to you we're zeroing in on a few places where he might live."

"I can't promise anything. This might involve Shannon. I can't stay still."

"I'll send you a mug shot. Later..."

Tower started hitting the computer keys. He was looking for a local address. He checked the phone and saw the incoming email from Mark David. The picture of Randall Solum brought everything back for Tower.

Solum had long hair. Long enough to cover most of his face. The strands went all the way down his back to the waist. The guy was heavy, weighing three-hundred-forty pounds at the time of his arrest. Tower remembered it all. The arrest of Solum came the very week Tower was by himself on patrol and no longer working with a training officer. Tower's first few days out on the street by himself. Solum represented a very large challenge. He resisted arrest and three other officers had to move in on the assist. Tower got the credit for the collar. The arrest was quick and Tower wasn't needed to testify at the trial.

Tower now had two, maybe three possible locations for where Solum was living. He picked up the phone and called Mark David.

"Yeah, Frank."

"Just an idea. And we don't have much time. What if we got in touch with the daughter, Reena. Maybe she could convince him to turn himself in. She could have all kinds of influence over him."

"We thought of that. That's a lead we can't pursue."

"Can't or won't? C'mon, Mark. His daughter must have been on his mind the whole time he was there. Just call her up."

"We can't, Frank. She died in a car crash the day before he was released from prison."

50

Tower put the phone down. Now, everything moved into sharp focus. His daughter Reena's death was his motive. Every move, every murder was connected to Reena. He could see why the victims were put at places where he would have been with his daughter, only he was in prison. They were all part of a death vengeance to be carried out across the city. A vengeance that wasn't over. Tower checked the countdown time:

02:14:19

He had just over two hours to find some trace of Ray, Shannon, or Jackie. Tower found one good address for Solum. His drive there was less than ten minutes. He got out to find a Stilton Bay police car out front. The female officer was walking back to her car.

"Ya get anything?"

"Frank Tower? I can't say anything to you directly, I'll get in trouble." She pulled out a notepad and wrote something down. She handed it to him. "Sorry I couldn't help you, Mr. Tower." She nodded to him.

For Tower, the nod meant read the note. She pulled away as Tower unfolded the piece of paper:

NO ONE LIVING HERE BY THE NAME OF RANDALL SOLUM

Tower surmised this was a location dump. Solum probably used this spot as a home address on any paperwork. A dead end.

He again called Shannon. No answer. Tower called the Never Too Late. Still no word from Jackie. When he tried Ray's Restaurant and got a busy signal, he drove there. There were five police cars out front. And Mark David.

"Frank, what are you doing here?"

"I'm just following up. I can't sit still."

"We got this, Frank."

"Then where is Ray?"

Mark David pointed to the front door. Ray was talking to Jake May. "He had to make a run to Miami to pick up some food items." David tried to block Tower from approaching Ray. "He ran out without his phone. Just got back a few minutes ago. He's okay. We're doing everything we can to find Shannon and Jackie. We've sent information to Miami-Dade police, Miami, Fort Lauderdale, and Broward County."

Tower moved in Ray's direction. A tug on his arm slowed him down. "Leave him alone, Frank. We're not going to let you talk to him right now. Just let it go."

"Does he know what's going on?"

"He does. We've made one discovery."

Tower stopped.

Mark David looked at the restaurant, then back to Tower. "He hired two employees a year ago."

"I remember him telling me. A cook and the clean-up man."

"Well, one of them is gone. He's missing. We did some checking, did a fingerprint check with prison records, and we came up with a match. We think he's our man."

"One?"

"Yes. One is here working. The other has been using a false name and is in the wind."

"So, who is it?"

51

Tower had to be restrained by Mark David one more time. The only thing Tower wanted to do was force his way inside the restaurant and look for him.

The clean-up man.

He was the very same man Tower helped up when Stan Brady knocked him down. The very guy Tower had spoken to and befriended as a worker at the best restaurant in the city.

"We're going through the guy's locker." Mark David finally got Tower to back down. "We think we found something. We're going through it now and we've got S.W.A.T. ready to move in somewhere. What I need you to do." Mark David paused to get Tower's full attention. "Listen to me. What I need you to do, Frank, is go back to your office. Stay out of our way. Don't listen to any police chatter. Go home. And wait. Let us handle this."

Tower was resigned to take his advice. He did a slow walk to his car and drove to the office. During the ride, he kept going over in his mind how Solum had changed. The man must have lost more than a hundred pounds. Instead of the long locks, this new version of Solum was bald. He had no prison tats. Kept himself clean. Tower just remembered the angry Solum, foul-mouthed and the smell of beer coming through his pores. His contact with him was a mere ninety minutes. After that, ten years of not thinking about Randall Solum. He could see how T.O. must have felt, dealing with old, discarded memories. He just looked like a different man.

Tower entered his office, throwing his keys on the desk. There, he went over the files emailed to him by Mark David that contained information on what Solum did in prison. Tower was ready to punch a giant hole in the wall as time was slipping away. He did a clock check.

00:47:29

Tower had less than an hour to figure out where they were. This wait for some word from Mark David was agonizing. He scanned through the information. Solum set himself up as a model prisoner by taking a few classes offered within the institution. He worked on several jobs including setting up speakers. The narrative described Solum as reading books on wiring and setting up sound systems. This was in accordance with his old job before going to prison of working the sound in dance clubs. Tower pushed away the laptop. He kept thinking, what was the name of the old dance club in Stilton Bay? The place was closed and boarded up for years.

Till Sunrise.

That was it. Till Sunrise. The place was south of the downtown district near three other empty warehouses. Stilton Bay's city council had been trying to figure out what to do with the properties for years. Old and deserted, only developers might have an idea on what to do with the spaces. Project ideas were raised, debated, and ultimately dropped.

Tower grabbed his keys.

He could drive by there and look around. Maybe that would take his mind off Mark David and the S.W.A.T. unit. Tower had faith in the police department. They would come through for him and Shannon. Three blocks into his drive, Tower thought he saw a car following him. The car kept up for a while, then slowed down and trailed off. Then nothing.

There were no cars in the vicinity.

00:03:10

Tower got out of the car and studied the area. His time was running out.

He was last here maybe three years ago, just driving through. The old dance club was boarded up. The double front entry doors had a thick chain wrapped around the panic bars. Tower made sure he had his Glock.

He checked two windows before he found one he could enter. Tower had no idea what he was doing. He just couldn't sit at the office and wait. He climbed up and inside the place. The smell of cooler, dry air permeated the large space. Till Sunrise was built like a small football stadium. Stairs led to upper levels where you could find a table and look down into the lower bowl. Up above, the lights were covered in cobwebs. Tower kept walking until he was on the dance floor. Memories of the place came back to him. The entire dance floor was metal. Large sheets of metal were bolted together, making up a unique dance area. All the speakers looked like they had been removed. Back in the day, some of the sound was connected by wires to the floor, and when the bass kicked in, you could feel the vibration in your feet. Dancers were literally part of the music. Moving bright lights from above would shine and glitter on the metal. The place used to rock.

Now, there was quiet.

Tower heard something.

The bits of noise came from the rear of the place, once reserved for the long hallway for waiters to deliver meals. The hallway led to the kitchen.

Tower followed the traces of noise.

He walked down the hallway and drew his Glock from the holster. Other than some graffiti, the walls were clean. Tower saw a door coming up on his left. When he reached it, he saw there were three locks. All of them looked new. He unbolted them and slowly opened the door. Inside the room, the smell of urine and fecal matter almost knocked him down. The space was empty. During his quick check, he saw a large speaker on either side of the door.

On the far wall, he saw a round smudge.

A woman uttered a muffled scream.

Tower kept going toward the kitchen double doors. Each door had a glass portal. Tower got close and attempted a peek. He could only see feet on a gurney. Tower eased one of the double doors open. As he moved inside the old kitchen, he could see who was on the gurney.

One person.

Jackie.

Her head was resting on something so she could see across the room. She was strapped down and unable to move. Tower searched her eyes and was convinced she was given some type of drug to make her easier to handle. On the wall were long knives and on the table there was sewing equipment. Suture thread. Before Tower took a step, a large figure walked up next to Jackie's head.

Solum.

He was wearing a mask. A black box was attached to his chest. He placed a sharp-bladed knife next to Jackie's throat. There were two pieces of thread pulling her lips together. He was in the process of sewing up her mouth.

"Ah, do come in." The voice was even and garbled. He sounded like a robot. "Please know, you do not want to use that weapon. I can very easily slice into her throat. And we don't want that, do we?"

"Let her go, Randall."

When he heard his name, he used his free hand to pull the mask and voicebox from his face. He was crouched down a bit behind the end of the gurney and Jackie, making it a difficult shot.

Solum adjusted the knife so a slice now would cut into Jackie's throat. "Put the gun down or I give her throat a new smile."

Tower resisted. "People are on the way. Step away from her."

"Her? You don't care about her, do you?"

"Just let her go." Tower took two small steps forward.

"Stop!" Solum barked the command. "There's no one coming. I saw you the second you got here."

He was right. Tower looked left and saw a bank of surveillance monitors. Three monitors showed video from just outside the building. Another was trained on the dance floor. He even installed a camera at Ray's Restaurant.

"Yes, I know about wiring. Wired this place. Did all the electrical for the club. And I heard about you and her."

Tower remained in place for the moment. "You haven't heard anything."

"I know how she treated you. Spent all the money on drugs and no food for you. All drugged up and left you alone."

"She's not like that now. She's helping people."

"C'mon, you want me to finish this. You don't give a damn about her. She's nothing to you, not even a best friend."

"She's worth saving. Her life now is giving a future to people about to go over the edge, Randall."

Jackie squirmed a bit under the knife. The words spewed from Solum like the hiss of a snake. "You move, Jackie, and this knife won't have to do any work. You'll cut yourself."

She tried to speak. "Taksh sha shot." Her words were distorted because of the two sutures tying her lips together.

Solum was smiling. "Look at her trying to say take the shot. Last time, Tower, put the gun down!"

Against everything he was trained to do, Frank Tower placed his Glock on the floor.

"Now kick it away."

Tower gave the weapon a kick, sending it sliding some ten feet away. Jackie stopped pushing against the restraints.

Solum stood up. The knife was still on Jackie's throat. "You're going to hear me out, Tower."

"No time. They'll be here any second."

"The police? They're not coming. I left enough stuff in my locker to send them in the wrong direction."

Tower figured the distance from himself to the gurney was fourteen feet. If he could just get Solum's attention on something else. "Some setup you have."

Solum's eyes stayed riveted on Tower. "The cameras? Yes. Even watched people crying at the memorial. I enjoyed every second of it. I want everyone connected to my conviction to suffer every day. I could easily kill each one, but why not kill the people most important to them? And watch them go through the pain I'm going through."

"Your daughter. And the car crash."

"I counted each day until I would get out. We could start all over. And then she was taken away from me. I've been suffering. My lawyer, the social worker, the judge. And you, Tower. You were the one who slapped the cuffs on me. Hauled me out right in front of my neighbors and my daughter, like some most-wanted idiot. I wanted you for last. I want you all to suffer every single day like I'm suffering without my daughter."

Tower took a chance. He slid his feet forward, moving even closer to the gurney. "I'm suffering, Solum. You made your point. Now let her go."

"I want to see her die. Like the rest. You don't care about her. Not her. She was a junkie. Just let her die like the best friends." Over his right shoulder, Tower saw what he meant. The photographs stolen from the homes. Pictures showing victims.

"When you posed those people, the pond, the pier, and the walking park..."

Solum cut him off. "Those are places I went with my daughter. My memories."

Tower moved a bit closer. "Only you didn't take her to those places. Your wife took her, not you. You were too busy drinking your beers and leaving rings of water on the table. Your wife didn't like it."

Two more quick steps forward.

"Damn woman. Made me mad. When I took these people, I took a swig on a beer and left the rings wherever I wanted." The grip on Jackie's throat eased. "I did want to take my daughter to those places. I thought about it every day in the joint. I was a model inmate. And then she died. Car crash. My whole world crashed. So I wanted everyone to feel my pain, especially you. I just want her to die and let you watch."

Tower rushed forward like a charging football lineman and put all of his weight into the thrust. He smashed his body into the end of the gurney, sending the thing crashing into Randall Solum. He fell backward and away from the gurney.

Tower had just seconds to move in on him. Solum got up, slashing at the air with the knife. Tower took up a defensive stance. He pushed the gurney away from them both and just missed a swipe aimed at his midsection. Another wild swing of the knife. Another close slice at his stomach. Tower was about to move inside Solum's swing. Then everything changed.

A gunshot.

The bullet hit the wall off Solum's right shoulder.

A miss.

The next one did not.

The shot hit Solum in the left chest. He was still upright and moving toward Tower. The next three shots hit Solum in the lower body and the top of his shoulder. He was reeling. Tower looked around.

T.O. had Tower's Glock.

She kept firing. Tower jumped to the side to make sure he was not in range. The gurney was a couple of yards away. Solum was able to keep standing until the next shot hit him in the forehead. He dropped to the ground.

His open eyes frozen in death.

T.O. kept pulling the trigger. Over and over. The bullets hit their mark, puffing up the clothing on a now-still Randall Solum. Loud bangs echoed in the room until there were just clicks.

Click, click, click, click.

In the calmest voice possible, Tower reached over and eased the gun out of T.O.'s hand. She was still pulling the trigger. She fell into Tower's chest, holding on to him. "I did it for Preston."

"That was you following me?"

"I stole Janine's car."

52

Tower tried, yet the paramedics would not let him get close to Jackie as they were checking her vitals. When they finished an initial run of her condition, the fire rescue truck left. Tower never had a chance to speak with her. And he was waiting for Mark David to grant him permission to leave the scene.

There were too many questions to answer first.

Mark David went first. "When we got to the location we knew it was a misdirection. We tracked your cell phone location and sent everyone here. Nice on your part to put it all together."

Tower turned to see them move Solum's body to the medical examiner's van. "I read his prison file. He was into wiring. It was Solum who set up this elaborate club. Then, I remembered it's been closed for years. I tried a hunch."

David rested a hand on his gun holster. "Solum was good at erasing his tracks. The attack on the judge's clerk, he had apparently cut the surveillance cameras the day before."

Tower watched a cadre of crime techs moving evidence bags out of the closed dance club. "What's going to happen to T.O.?"

"Well, the final call will be up to the state attorney's office, but we're recommending no charges. It was self-defense, right?"

"Solum was about to carve me up. Yeah, it was self-defense. She was protecting me and herself."

"And Jackie."

"Yes, Jackie."

Mark David tucked his notepad into the belt of his pants. "And T.O. won't be charged with car theft. Janine Iwan doesn't want to press charges."

Frank Tower picked up a chunk of soil and tossed it away. "You know, I looked right at Solum at the restaurant and I didn't recognize him."

"No one did. He lost more than a hundred-fifty pounds in prison, lost his long hair, the beard, everything. The techs say he was even wearing brown contact lenses. His eyes are a gray color."

Tower grabbed more soil. "I remember busting him now. I had just left rookie status and it was my first week alone. First week. That arrest was a blur."

"The problem is he's been thinking about that arrest every day. We think he's had a year to plan out the killings. He used the mask to avoid facial rec. And stole an identity as Stacker."

"My wife, Shannon?"

"She's fine. She can tell you all about it."

Mark David walked over to Jake May and two other detectives. A woman approached him from the right.

Leandra Crosland was wearing business slacks, a lavender blouse, and white shoes. "You okay?"

"The question is, how are you?"

"Going back to school. Finishing up my degree in fashion design."

"Good for you."

She looked around. "I followed the TV crews. Word travels fast. Stan is going to testify against Nat. Stan will still do some time but he'll be okay." She kicked at the dirt with her shiny white shoes. "I want to apologize to you."

"For what?"

"All the spitting. And the way I treated you. That was the old Leandra. You take care, Frank Tower." She turned and walked with a purpose.

Two hours later, after giving a statement, Tower was released to go home.

53

Shannon Tower couldn't stop smiling. "So, I get to the airport and find out someone had stolen my cell phone. Right out of my purse. Got distracted. But thanks to police, and some quick work, I got it back. But I missed my flight. You miss me?"

Tower moved in and kissed her again for the twentieth time since he saw her. "I always miss you."

"They told me this guy said I was kidnapped?"

"We didn't know what to think." Tower leaned in again and kissed her on the cheek.

"Okay, that's enough. And what are we doing?"

Tower opened the car door, walked around, and let her out in front of Ray's Restaurant. "This is our destination. Ray's. I've got a special guest coming."

"A special guest. And I'm not special?"

They both laughed.

Inside, at his usual spot, the table with the view of the street and the front door, Tower gave a menu to Shannon. "I know what I want."

Ray walked to their table and Tower posed a question like an open-liner in a stand-up routine. "So, Ray, how are you doing?"

"I'm happier than a fully-fed bird hovering over a cleanest car convention."

Before the laughter waned, someone walked into the restaurant.

Jackie Tower.

She looked around the place, found Frank and Shannon, and immediately put a hand over her mouth where the sutures and thread were removed in the hospital.

Tower got up and greeted her at the table.

Then, he did something he hadn't done since he was twelve years old, when he ran away from home, vowing to never return because of all the drug use he witnessed. Not since the series of missed meals when no food was brought into the house, only drugs wrapped in foil, and three times she broke a promise to stop taking drugs after withdrawal attempts. Not since he swore he had been through so much shit he could never, ever again address her by the M word.

Until now.

Frank Tower hugged Jackie.

She looked at the floor. Tower took his finger and put it under her chin, making her look up. "Ray, she's never been here before, and even though you lived close by I don't think you two ever talked. I want you to meet my mother."

AUTHOR'S NOTE

I love Stilton Bay for all its beauty and charm. It is home for P.I. Frank Tower. Please know, Stilton Bay is the creation of the author. I did try to bring to life the exotic radiance of South Florida, the locale of the book.

ABOUT THE AUTHOR

For many years, Mel Taylor watched history unfold as he covered news stories in the streets of Miami and Fort Lauderdale. A graduate of Southern Illinois University, Mel writes the Frank Tower Private Investigator series. He lives in a community close to one of his favorite places – The Florida Everglades. South Florida is the backdrop for his series.

Printed in the United States
by Baker & Taylor Publisher Services